PURPLE

PURPLE

R. MARK PEARD

ARCHWAY
PUBLISHING

Archway Publishing books may be ordered through booksellers or by contacting:

Archway Publishing
1663 Liberty Drive
Bloomington, IN 47403
www.archwaypublishing.com
1 (888) 242-5904

ISBN: 978-1-4808-5863-3 (sc)
ISBN: 978-1-4808-5864-0 (e)

Library of Congress Control Number: 2018901754

Print information available on the last page.

Archway Publishing rev. date: 2/22/2018

To my wife Kimberly
who stood by me through illness and
gave me patience and strength

CHAPTER 1

A dark, cold, and rainy night settles on the redwood forest floor to await the morning sun that will break through the forest morning mist. The soft chilling breeze wanders through the trees just enough to brush off the dewy rain that lies on the leaves. The stars shone bright twinkling in the black night sky.

Kyle and Frank's sweat runs down their faces mixing with the drizzling rain as they struggle with the awkward weight of the lifeless body. The body is less than a struggle for Kyle with his six-foot plus frame than Frank.

"This is your idea of a place to dump the body?" Frank says, in frustration.

"Not dump but place it in a place where it can be seen" Kyle responds in a short whisper.

"Place it where? On this gravel parking area, and then lets get out of here" Frank says in a loud whisper, and adds "We are going to get caught, that is what is going to happen".

Kyle struggles with the wet rain soaked body while holding the mag light.

"I just want to get it on top of the granite marker; now, give me a hand before his clothes get soaked!" Kyle says, in an angry whisper, and "don't let the body drag on the rocks and dirt, and keep your gloves on".

Kyle goes behind the marker to get a footing, placing the body on the ledge of the eight-foot marker. Frank positions the body so that Kyle can lift it to the edge of the marker ledge and pushes the body up to Kyle. Kyle hoists the body up to the ledge of the Marker and looks out to the west of the Marker and can see Derrick's greenhouse in the far distance with the fire raging and can almost hear the glass roof and sides crashing on the floor.

"See I told you we could do two jobs in one night. 'Dirty deeds done cheap' Kyle says with an evil chuckle – "we earned ourselves some pretty coin tonight to spend", Kyle says patting himself on the back and continues "…I got just the evidence to point the finger at Derrick for the death of this guy".

He takes out a flower from his shirt pocket and places it inside the jacket pocket of the body. Kyle jumps down and high fives Frank with a big grin. As they leave, they kick at the gravel rocks in the parking lot trying to get rid of any tracks they may have left behind, and Kyle takes a walk backwards to their 4x4 to look that everything has been set right

"Ok I think the rain will erase any tracks – think we are ok to go" Kyle says.

Frank exclaims "lets get out of here this place is giving me the creeps and doing two jobs is just pushing our luck too far, damn you!"

They speed off to the sounds of popping granite stones under the weight of the tires and are swallowed up by the darkness and the little rain that seemed fitting for the nights work.

Kyle is anxious as Frank drives away in the pickup from the Park's side Entrance.

"Let's swing by Ron's casino, I need a drink", Kyle exclaimed to Frank as they speed on the highway away from the Marker.

"Now you are talking" Frank responds cheerfully and continues, "the casino is opened past midnight, maybe if Ron is there we can get paid".

"You know Ron does not do any business in the casino", Kyle responds and adds, "we did the job and Ron has never stiffed us. Just be patient he will want to wait and make sure we did it right and there are no problems. Now put that tarp over the marijuana plants in the truck bed and take special care of the one with PURPLE leaves and I'll look for a parking spot away from everything".

Kyle and Frank had quite the haul for a night's works.

The Casino is on the main highway and is a quick 20-minute drive from the Marker. Ron, the Casino owner, meets Kyle and Frank at the front entrance of the Casino in a turned down collar suit and says before they could tell Ron about the haul they hear

Ron say "Maybe you boys should go clean up before you come into the Casino". Ron continues, "maybe you should come back tomorrow. Watch out for the Sheriff Lee and his sidekick deputy Donnie. It's raining just enough to make the highway wet and slippery so they will probably be out".

Kyle and Frank look at themselves and decide not to make a fuss and head off to go to Kyle's moms store, Shara's Flower Shop, which is a 30-minute drive north up the highway.

"Well that's a bummer, guess we are uninvited". As they walk back to the car, Frank says to Kyle angry at not getting into the casino to check out the girls.

Kyle quickly responds, "It is just as well with all we have done tonight I would be too nervous to gamble and I don't think I could think straight anyway."

Frank responds, "I guess you are right, maybe we should stop by and see Sally." Frank suggests.

"She is spending the night with Kiki – girl stuff you know; how is Joe doing"? Kyle asks,

"Think my old man is running a load of logs again" Frank responds and adds, " he is still after me to join up at the Mill, lets head over to your place, that way maybe we can run over to Ron's tomorrow morning".

Back at the casino Ron turns to the doorman and says, "Let me know if ED Falconer or his assist Michael show up. They are from the QUANTEX Company. Don't let anyone else in we are about to close up and especially don't let any of those damn marijuana dealers in that you don't know, and no Tweekers those damn speed freaks no telling what they will do".

※　※　※　※　※

The next day the early morning air smelled fresh and new and with a bit of smoldering fire somewhere.

"Donnie, I hear there was a fire over at Derrick's place in his greenhouse and it sounds suspicious. Think I will go over there and take a look", Lee says as he leaves the station.

Lee calls Derrick on his cell phone but there is no answer "guess he must be busy with the fire people" Lee thinks to himself.

The fire was still smoldering with the acrid odors of a dying fire, with water soak burning wood that seemed to fill the air. As Lee pulls up pulled up to the greenhouse, Lee gets out and greets Derrick, they both stand outside of Derrick's greenhouse with only framing left. Most of the greenhouse was gone even the roof, a total loss except for one small corner where just a touch of green could be seen that catches Derrick's eye. Lee appears to be focused on the damage while Derrick climbs into the smoldering wreck of a building through the broken windows.

"Watch yourself" Lee shouted.

While Derrick tries to slip away into the smoldering mess of what used to be his greenhouse. Derrick wraps a bandana around his nose and mouth and ties it in the back of his head.

"Maybe we should wait until the Fire Chief gets here" Lee adds

Watching Derrick closely, trying to be a concerned friendly 'Sherriff'. But Derrick isn't having any of it and hastens carefully through the broken glass that crunch beneath his lug boots; the acrid smoke fills the air and his bandana.

"It will be ok!" Derrick says breathlessly trying not to raise any unwanted concerns. "Just want to get to this corner, I thought I saw something that needed to be rescued before the clean up started" Derrick replies coughing from the smoldering odors.

"OK, I'll watch out for you from over here" Lee replies in a matter of fact way shaking his head trying to be understanding. Derrick reaches the sooty green plants that are in the corner and he cups the plant in his hand and makes his way back towards Lee. There is a mess of plants mostly out of the black plastic pots scattered on the floor. Derrick looks at the damaged plants and thought what a loss as he picks up a purple bud up from the floor lying on the broken glass and stuck it in his pocket. As he bent down looking under the growing tables, he could see the signs of a broken entryway through the glass window – the glass looks to be broken from the outside coming inward. Derrick shakes his head with a smile and made his way back to where Lee is.

Covered in soot, Derrick holds the plant and says "here hold this for me. … Here is something for your troubles."

As he hands the PURPLE bud to Lee, Derrick with a sooty smile, crunching the broken glass beneath his boot where he stood, places the small plant in Lee's hand appears to be some kind of plant that Lee guesses is some type of orchid similar to the ones that he had seen in Sarah's shop.

Derrick tells Lee, it was a rare orchid he found on a trip to South America. Lee sniffed the orchid flower, a sweet smell like some sort of perfume. He explained, "I need a place to get it back in shape; like a plant or orchid hospital" Derrick quipped back to him. " So you lost a beautiful rare plant; can you save it?" Lee asks.

"Oh I have many others just no more space and I lost al lot of them in the fire". Derrick responds.

CHAPTER 2

JOE LOGS AND DEER

There is the lightest of rain falling, a gentle mist that settles lightly on the ferns with droplets falling silently on the leaves that settle on the forest floor. The presence of the stillness of damp time could be felt through out the forest. A forest thick with Pine and Fir filled the musty smell of trees long dead and gone. In among the Pine and Fir a few Hardwood Sycamore and Poplar could be seen as they struggled with the altitude; and there…the ever so often a redwood could be found standing proud and stately. The forest surrounds everything and brings a hush that envelops the whole of Emerald. Loggers once disturbed the forest hush and clear-cut the redwoods long ago … now stands no older than 50-75 years old were all that the forest could offer. But for some that know where to look for them, and Joe, Frank's father, knows just where to look.

Early morning and Joe wakes from his night in the forest, sleeping in his big semi-tractor cab; waiting for the time when all is black in the forest and the hush returns to the forest with a misty fog. Joe had hiked deep into the forest the day before, during the late wet afternoon - keeping a careful watch to see if anyone is about. The BLM (Bureau of Land Management) federal cops like to hide out or patrol the fire roads whenever they get a tip about logs being cut or hauled. His big semi-with its trailer load of logs is parked in a small forest clearing just off the fire road; just where it should be. Joe got out of the truck, stretches and takes a walk about round the trailer, pounding his hands against the straps and pulling at the chains that hold the mighty logs in place. The forest is whisper quiet and pitch black. After a careful stare into the blackness and he listens for any unusual or unnatural sounds, he hears the rev of a small 4x4 engine. Joe turns back towards the semi and climbs into the sleeper cab behind the seats. He listens carefully at what direction the noise is coming from – could be any one of many things BLM Feds, marijuana growers coming to get to their camp for tomorrows watering or people just chasing a "WHO DO go there", Joe tells himself

He hears the sounds subside in a going away sound – and thinks it must be someone getting out of my way probably some growers in the area. Joe waits until the sound is gone from the evening blackness and figures that they must be far enough off of the main fire road to get going. The roar of his large Semi-tractor engine breaks the silences of the forest, as he starts up the mighty diesel engine. Soon he feels the warmth of the engine as it slowly wakes from its slumber. Joe sits and smokes a marijuana joint while he waits for the engine to warm. He thinks of his boy Frank and where he might have gone off to and hopes that he stays out of trouble. Frank and Joe had a big fight the night that Frank left. He had been talking about dealing some new weed called PURPLE due to its purple color leaves – rumor has it that the strain had over 40% THC.[1]

The highest ever recorded and the plant would make an ideal commercial plant stock just need the right Pharmacy company. But Joe told him it is too risky and he wanted no part of it in his house. Joe thinks to himself Marijuana is still illegal and Joe wanted no part of it; a new weed called PURPLE with 40% THC

"Yeah right" Joe mumble under his breath and a new weed called PURPLE it is probably mixed up with some smart gang people like Ron, who runs the casino I just don't want any part of it.

Angrily Joe slams the gears in place, turns on his low running lights, slowly making his way on to the main fire road and out into the damp rocky forest road out onto the highway. The tractor tires argue under Joe's frustration and

[1] Tetrahydrocannabinol is the principal psychoactive constituent (or cannabinoid) of canna-bis./ marijuana.

spin under the weight of the trailer's load of large freshly cut lodge pole pine and younger redwoods; the redwoods make Joe particularly nervous.

It's illegal to cut trees on the Bureau of Land Management (BLM) forestlands and there are large fines and jail time for cutting redwoods. But Joe, like some others will take the risk during harder times – after all the forest had belonged to the "real" families - the ones that were here before BLM took the forest away. 'preservation' they were told – but most think of it as government thievery for the rich logging companies… for the big logging companies are the only ones that can afford the government lease cost, to cut timber on the BLM land.

The black of the night keeps Joe's speed down as he heads out off the fire road on to the old Castle Road- part asphalt and part potholes. The wipers slapping with dirty streak across the windshield as he splashes through the potholes and he could hear the logs pressing against their chains as he made the turns.

Joe reaches for the radio knob - then suddenly the truck jolted to the left and the wheel turns to one-side; he held on tight to the steer 'n wheel as it pulled – he could feel the trailer sliding.

"What the hell" Joe yells out; as he quickly took his foot off the pedal and grabs the gear-shift.

"Bessie" grumbles and shook at her displeasure – like being awaken from a pleasant morning nap.

He gears Bessie down and hits the airbrakes – tires grabbing at the road close to the shoulder - the logs pressing against the chains and Joe could feel the weight of the load pushing him forward. Bessie pulls and Joe pulls harder as he settled her to a stop on the gravel shoulder. Joe's heart still pounding as he looks back at the blackness in his side mirror, a blackness that could swallow a man whole - he could still hear Bessie in his head as she grumbled and shook to a stop along the narrow shoulder. Joe takes another look in the mirror into the blackness.

This is the "narrows" – the truckers call it - where the two-lanes just squeeze at you, as part of the highway, just nowhere to move. You just never know who or what is going to be out there, he thought, as he gathers his mind and turns back in his seat to grab his jacket and tire-thumper, mag light from behind the seat.

Joe is short of stature but built like a bowling ball as they'd say. He'd just laugh and say "it got me through Nam" – yep there is not much that would scare off Joe. He steps out from the tractor cab and jumps off the step. As he looks back along the trailer in the dark morning, he snaps up his jacket. He could already feel the cold night air cutting right through him and his threadbare jeans. He walks to the front of tractor and inspects the front and could see what looked like blood – and thought 'Damn it better not be a hitcher'. Joe's heart sunk as he thought of his son, Frank, that had run off about a year ago now.

He walks on around the tractor on to the gravel that crackles under his boots - he stops at the passenger's side-door of the cab; Joe's breath hung in the air as he yells out into the darkness; "HEY…!" the same 'hey' he would use on a dog as well as a man.

Joe shines the Mag light into the darkness but the light is swallow whole. He could hear a sound and a snort as he walked closer, the light caught a shadowy movement of something lying on the road, up a little passed where the logs hung pass the trailer. "Damn deer" Joe yells out as if talking to the highway and it is talking back to him.

Deer in early winter were the worst of the trucking hazards at night. They could take out a car going 70 on the flats; turn it over just to spite the driver, and then die like some bee that had taken one for the troops in the process.

Joe walks back toward the movement and sees a young buck struggling to get up; "Damn…!" Joe mumbles under his breath as he walks closer. Joe took a look at the steel tire thumper in his hand and thought of the rifle in the truck as he stood over the struggling buck. He shakes his head at the young buck and grips the steel tire thumper harder.

"Just not your day" and says "via con Diaz, young one."

Joe swings the steel rod down hard at the buck's head and the steel hook cracks into the buck's skull, he could hear the cracking sound of bone as the hook-end cracks open the buck's skull. Joe quickly swung two more times, as the buck lays motionless, just to make sure. The deer's blood splattered across his pant legs, face and hands. "Damn – just in the wrong place" Joe says to himself. "Well at least the wolfs and coyotes will eat well – "free meal...!" he yells into the blackness.

Joe could feel the buck's blood on his face and looks down at the blood spatter on his pants - "DAMN" he thinks, well the rest stop is just up the way.

Joe pulls the deer carcass further back on the shoulder of the road and he walks slowly back on the passenger side of his rig; in the darkness, feeling fortunate there is no one on the road. As Joe steps up on to his cab steps pieces of deer flesh, blood and bone fall down on the step. He opens the passenger door, throws the tire-thumper on the cab floor, and grabs the water container from under the passenger seat and washes off his hands. The water felt warm against the cold of the night. Joe looks off to the East, he could see the clouds breaking; and a thousand million stars dancing in the blackness – 'now that is what the tourist should come for' and then thinks of the young bucks spirit crossing the night sky like some comet in the sky.

Joe knocks his boots against the step and walks around the tractor and slid into the cab; "OK 'ol girl – we got 'miles to go before we sleep' or something like that" he says to himself.

Joe pulls out onto the highway and left the Terryville flats in the blackness of the night. He gears up and puts his boot to the floor knowing the road is flat for a bit and offers some rest – he turns the radio knob

"...*Fat bottom girls -You make the rocking' world go round...*"

The local station is finally com'n in strong and clear – or at least clear enough for old Bessie's radio. The radio station had been one of the "offerings" from the growers. Before the radio station there was nothing cept Country Music and some Bluegrass now and then; but this station pumps out pure ol' time rock & roll.

As Joe let the road ease his mind and his ears fill with rock n' roll passing by mountain fir and pine trees, he thinks of the days, like it use to be back not too far away.

That first group of Hippies, they were a smart group of college kids coming up this way - mostly running from the draft on their way to Canada. But some stay and settle in the woody backcountry with rolling pastures and groves of redwood and pine; he thinks how the parent's money helped most. Some stay cuz they thought they could make a difference; teaching, cuz there isn't any real schools for the local kids, for most local kids either left or went into farming after schooling. Those Hippies were sure full of ideas - even formed groups to help each others, Communes they called them, he thought- but work is hard to come by and most locals didn't want them around; so most of them left. The ones that stayed found they needed real money to make a difference and started growing marijuana weed for sale to the tourist; first a little here and there – but then it started to make' n real money but when the locals found out then the real trouble started. Nobody wants the hippies around with there "we are all brothers mentality", they just did not seem to fit in with the community. But the hippies became real farmers – Marijuana Growers – and found they had money enough to really make a difference but everything they "offered or sponsored" seemed to have a price and a purpose in their needs – it isn't just doing things cuz they needed to be done.

In the early days after the "Summer of Love" had past, and the pseudo hippies had left the scene Joe thought, the real organized grow'n got started - but so did the Nixon War on Drugs. In these parts the war on drugs was serious business with Feds, Marshals, County Sherriff's and the locals they all were too serious. Helicopters swoop 'n around, they were the worse. They would drop in on them with only a few minutes notice – oh you could hear the chopper com' n a ways off but that didn't give the new locals much time to scramble. These kids found out farming were real work and found that their crops needed serious tending from rabbits, rats, ranchers cows and the like. Then a small group got together to start building a warning system and their own radio station was born.

Individuals would call in the directions and speed of the sheriff choppers into the radio station, and they had the additional benefit that many of the early growers were Vets from Nam. The station would broadcast co-ordnance "two copters seen coming east off Eagle Point going slow to the west" then right down the community line all the way to the fields so everybody knew. The system gave them valuable time to harvest and run, scatter or just lay low. That way everyone got a chance to do what he or she had to do. Then the Feds stepped in with the FCC and caused some legal issues, costing the growers dearly.

'Man that must of cost 'em a year crop' Joe thought.

Then there is the small dirt airstrip that the growers built. That brought more Feds and the FAA then stepped in for airport safety they say; but all the legal battles just made the real growers more determined - that was when the grower's cooperative is formed, and small groups of growers formed as stakeholders. Every grower knew that they had to join in on the fight; no matter the cost. All their growing profits went into that airstrip and the radio station making everything legal and Fed certified. Those that did make some profit had to distribute it amongst the group - that was the pack they made in those early days.

* * * * *

The dark morning sky fills with stars and the road soon enough turns into a highway and Joe turns up the radio;

"I is just a skinny lad - Never knew no good from bad"

Joe didn't much care for the song but its rock & roll and the sound is coming from where he is going. Joe sat back in his seat and watched as the two lane highway became a real four lane highway; It had been built and finished soon after the '72 flood which helped to get supplies in and people out and help prepare for the next flood.

Joe could see that the misty rain was letting up and in the distant Backcountry mountains the sliver of a moon gave a peace and beauty that belies the backcountry. The stars challenge the moon for their own place and the mountain fog lay soft and calm in the mountain gaps. Joe thinks about all the silliness he'd been thinking back on the road, and shook his head, putting his boot to the floor and geared up preparing for the climb through the "Rattle Snake" grade.

The mist returns and begins to thicken as he climbs, wipers quicken their slapp'n while Joe pours himself the last of his coffee; "least it warm" Joe grumbles. The radio crackles and fades as if to warn of the road ahead. Joe can feel the climb of the grade; oh it is manageable for Bessie, the road is not like it used to be. The radio dies as Joe hit the front south side of Rattle Snake grade and he flips the knob over to the CD as Willey Nelson came through,

Joe looks at his speed "still hold's 60" – "that's it babe, you know the way" he whispers to himself as they crossed the Twin Peak summit.

Joe eases his grip on the wheel and geared for the decent, he knows going down from the summit would be another sort of trouble; and that the real driving lay ahead as the highway hugs the "Rattle Snake" river, for which it has earns its name - tight twisting curves and mountain walls that squeeze the Highway back to two lanes or less with signs of 'Watch for Falling Rock'.

Joe mumbles to himself "…by the time you see a falling rock – it's too late."

Joe remembers when they had to shut down the section of the highway for a boulder as big as a house – the big old Rock is just there laid on the highway. There is no getting around the "Rattle Snake" river – that river owns this part of the backcountry. The road here is just a little piece of the backcountry to remind you that you have to work and earn your peace to stay here. For the growers the Rattle Snake is almost ideal; it meant they could see anyone coming. Little side roads dot the Rattle Snake, going off to back country for fish'n the Back River holes, and off to locked bar road gates that blocked roads where the growers have easy access to the highway.

Joe slows way down for Pratt's Place, where the two lane road squeezes so tight, that trucks going either way would have inches or less between them; and the shoulder is a steep canyon wall on one side and a 300 foot drop on the other. This is a trucker's nightmare road, and forget about an over-sized load there is a special nasty fee to pay for having to shut the Rattle Snake down through this stretch; there is just no other way around, less'n you felt like a 100 mile detour.

Joe hears Bessie argue as he gears down further and Joe hugs the mountainside. He could just hear the log chains bumping and scraping the "<u>Watch for falling Rocks</u>" signs as he went by them. Joe looks back but the sign seems none-the-worst for ware. Joe knew that leav'n the Rattle Snake means almost the last of the trouble of getting in to Emerald.

As Joe got ready to leave the Rattlesnake, the mountain took its final shot by sticking itself out two foot into the road; Joe could hear the chains scrap 'n against the rock. The Army Core had left the over-hang stay cause the 'old log'n trucks could fit fine underneath it. Joe eases up a bit as he left the Rattle Snake – and looks down at the 300 ft drop that the Rattle Snake had carved - he knew the Rest stop is just ahead.

There is only one real rest stop around for miles – a peaceful place with the forest all around and critters running about rabbit and gray squirrels. During the summer there would be truckers and tourist folks alike coming out of the back country – most sitting around on the park benches trading stories of where to go and …not go! Oh, there isn't much real trouble with the growers these days not like there used to be - Back in the Day when growers would take pot shots at anyone com'n anywhere near their crop; without any warning – well it isn't like you could put up a sign "Keep out - Pot Farm". But things have settled down quite a bit as the growers got more organized and a kind of peace pack is in place – nothing in writing just a general understanding.

Joe swings the big log rig around left, and enters the Rest Area not many people about at 4am except truckers. Joe jumps out of his rig and heads for the facilities to wash up; felt good to get a chance to stretch after the Rattle Snake. You can feel the cold of the mountain air; as your breath held in the air. A trucker with his hair fallen out from under his cap gave a glance at Joe as he passed him, looking down at his pant leg and boots splatter with blood that glistened from the over-head night lights. Joe just says "Deer – near Terryville" the passer-by just gives a nod of acknowledgement and understood it's just how things happen on the highway in these parts.

Joe got as much of the blood as he could off his boots, but he isn't about to sit in his truck with wet jeans so he just let that part be – just a little deer blood. Joe hopped back into his rig; the trailer kick'n gravel as the big logs bounced when he pulls out and heads north. Joe tips his cap back and knows it would be a gentle drive (a tourist type road) as he enters the "Grove" and flipped the radio back on and hears

"*…well, someone called in a spotters helicopter – fly 'n high; he must be fly 'n high cause it's raining here folks."*

Joe looks up but the sky is black with clouds - filled with that look, like they are about to give an irritating drizzle – the kind you'd just wish it would rain. "They won't be flying in this weather" – Joe chuckles under his breath and kicks at the heater, think 'n again about that joint in the ashtray. There would be time enough for that; too cold and wet and I'll bet that wind up there would give them helicopters something to think about besides pot growers. The helicopters' have taken to flying at night because of the 'Growing Houses'; and Joe chuckles to himself.

Joe pulls back his sleeves, settles into the smooth ride and begin to grin think 'n how sometime back-in-the-day someone got the bright idea of building a grow 'n house – just an empty house with no rooms. It looked just like a wood pine in the redwood's house in the Backcountry Mountain woods; curtains on the widows, nice doorway, lights over the doorway and all the trimmings. But open the door and all you could see is square footage of marijuana pants, full of Emerald's finest - nice sticky buds - smelling fine, with full irrigation, ventilation and bright sodium lights. Oh the set up has been tried and failed many times, cuz tending to it and keeping six and ten foot plants healthily enough to full bud, well that takes labor and lots of it – trimming and bug chasing. It isn't till Derrick & Paul came up with the Emerald Dwarf; and that just did the trick - short squatty plants, loaded with sweet sticky buds and a better THC content – all crystal 'd out on the buds. Paul & Derrick could have made big money from their new plants - however, as had been agreed, they shared the new plants with the group – but just for the first year - then leasing or sold them to all the paying members of the

'Group' yep they made quite a name for themselves not that they really need to. All the sudden the community of growers had a year round crop and the backcountry specially Emerald had a construction housing boom; of course as agreed, housing property taxes and revenues were paid to the county – it is one of those win-win situation for everyone.

The outdoor growing dropped to only the small growers just starting out; and they couldn't get any help from the big growers less they pay the co-opt entry and monthly fees. But of course the Feds notice the increase in construction and housing, the reported tax revenue growth and that there is more pot than ever; with fewer busts. Then of course the census taker came round- but they never got quite what they were looking for. One time when the drought hit the cities, the bureaucrats started looking for underground streams and ponds, and they knew the Emerald Mountains had plenty of that. They came looking for water in their helicopters with spotting equipment and they found water but not where it should be. Nothing seemed to make sense to them until one of those water-searching helicopters was late coming in and read on their scanner that there is a pool of water where a house should be. And the war is on again. It is easy for the Feds lots of money available from the 'war on drugs'.

The big growers insulate the inside of the roof with foil but it is expensive except for the big growers; and the Feds added a night helicopter watch. It is only by the grace of the county sheriffs taking over the program that any grown got done. But of course there has to be some bust to keep the Feds happy and who better than those pesky start ups with no connection – the growers now had rules with some teeth – pay the price or risk get turned in. This didn't sit well with some, so off to Oregon, Washington and Canada they went... where it is more like it used to be – live and let live.

CHAPTER 3

THE GRANITE MARKER

Before Joe knows it, he is in EMERALD on the first Barber town entrance by the old motel. He feels the grumble of his stomach and thought he really didn't have time to stop. He thinks to himself 'Sally has just started working at the café; oh well its 5am still… dark but the clouds would be break'n soon. Have to stop in on the way back and see her; just a young pretty local gal with a smile that well … reminds him of Diane – and what a smile". A smile crept across Joe's face but he decides to keep speed down just a bit as he drives past the second Barber town entrance. He gives the town a blast from the diesel horn and thinks 'not much of a chance them really hear him cause of the hill between the town and the highway'. Joe kept that smile and thought 'it would sure be nice to see young Sally and that smile; maybe I'll catch her when her when her shift ends, sure would be nice'. Joe shook his head and thinks she's too young but oh so cute '…better get back into the drive'n and the *"…ain't no sunshine …"* came in to fill the cab. Joe slaps the wheel keep'n time to the music with a smile, as the radio station is coming in strong.

Joe checks his speed as the highway rounds the slow gentle bends of the Pike River, the road hugs the river's every lazy turn - flat and banked just enough – yep this is Emerald he thought. But Joe could see the rain is pick'n up again in the North – winter is coming - he could just begin to see the spray kicking up from the trailer wheels and thinks he better slow it down a bit more – that deputy likes to hang out around about here. Joe is heading into to the real Redwoods; pretty country; the kind that makes you want to whisper as you travel through it. "I'll make it to the mill by 6-7am no need to push my luck" he says to himself in a whisper as he settles back in his seat, and watches the wheel spray traveled behind him. "We'll…" Joe's words fade as he looks over at the Park entrance and it's Giant ten foot Granite marker up ahead on the left. It looked like someone is sitting on the Granite marker's top step – "someth'n only a local would do". Joe thought, who'd be out in this, as he sees the rain start'n to pick up again.

Joe slows Bessie way down to get a better look at who or whatever it is; Joe's son Frank had ran off about a year ago and he always held out some hope that he'd see him in town or on the road hitching. Joe put on the brakes sliding his rig as he pulls off on to the wide gravel highway shoulder – pick'n up hitchers is against the company rules – but this is Joe's tractor. Joe made the turn into the large parking entrance lot …the truck hit the gravel and he could hear the pop and scrap of the granite against the weight of the logs as he bounced in his seat. The Park service had wanted to pave the entrance due to the mud and dirt problems. One Monday morning the Rangers came in normal as they always do - and sees that the large front gravel dirt area that they were going to pave - had pretty blue and pink quarter size granite rock laid down at the entrance right up to the Park's large Granite Marker. No one ever said a word but everyone knew where the gravel had come from.

Joe pulls his rig as close as he can to the front of the Marker, Joe rolls down the passenger side window and yells "Hey want a lift, looks like it's get'n bad", but there is no response. 'No way someone would be sleep'n stoned in this weather; maybe he's hurt' Joe thought as he gave out another yell "HEY"; but no response. "Shit", Joe yelled to himself and reached for his rain slicker and the tire thumper from the under the passenger seat; and thinks this better not be no half dead drugged out stoner or Tweekers – those damn speed freakier. " I don't need this," he says to himself as he looked up and sees the mist turning to rain. The park entrance area is wide, cleared out area bordered by the forest trees, with just the

10 foot Granite Marker that marks the park side trail entrance with a brass plate map showing the area that could be seen easily from the road. The tourist sure liked it … almost like it points the way for them with the map inscribed in the Brass.

The cab door creaks as Joe opens it and he winces at the falling rain. Joe jumps down from the truck step and snaps up his slicker, pull's the hood over his head. He walks around the front of his tractor…griping the gray steel thumper …walking causally toward the large granite marker where the man is sitting up high on it. And yells again "HEY – you need some help…" as he loosens the grip on the thumper and bends down – to get a better look. He could see he still had blood on his pant leg from the deer. Joe looks from side to side trying to see if he could see the man's face. Joe yells again in a voice that just cleared the sound of the falling rain "Hey, you need some help"?

As Joe got closer and looks up at the man he could see the man's hands were an ashen purplish color. Joe bent down and looked up cautiously to see the man face. "Damn it…" Joe yells out "your dead - Son of a Bitch". Joe isn't one to hold back when he is pissed off. He kicks at the pink granite rocks, as he turns to one-side. "Shit now what", Joe says under his breath, as he walked about back and forth in front of the dead man. It isn't as if Joe hadn't seen a dead person before, he seen plenty in Nam, and locals around in Emerald. But the dead locals were usually in the river, fields, or hang'n in some empty apartment or warehouse, as he thinks to himself. Last month before the rains Joe had helped the Coroner pull out some guy and gal from the Pike River; then there was that girl they found hanging in her apartment living room with her baby crying just below her dangling feet a few months back; some say she is manicuring marijuana leaves and talked too much. Rumor was she worked for Ron but nothing could be proved. Ron always had the best attorneys and the girl is not well known in the area. Just another poor soul caught up in some bad stuff.

"How the hell did you get up there…"Joe yells to himself and then stops in mid sentence and realizes the only way the man could have gotten up the step …

that had been carved into the granite some 10 feet off the ground; is if someone to has put him there. Joe crouches and starts to look around at trees, around the park entrance; but he couldn't see nothing but trees blowing in the wind and rain - and all he could hear is the drone of the rain pounding against his hood and the gravel. And thought, 'well if there's anyone about they'd have me by now'.

The dead man is perched on the step just like anyone would be that knew this rock; sitting up straight but with his head bent down and water pouring off the brim of his hat (one of those wide brim adventure hats that have become so popular). Joe looks closer at the corpse – he is dressed like some local but the clothes look new, the hat looks like nice leather, red plaid shirt and a brown water soaked leather vest and what looks to be new blue-jeans and new lug boots – but no rain gear or jacket. "Shit, Damn, Fuck… there goes a fucking load and probably the day bonus" he yells out.

Joe walks back to his tractor cursing and kicking at anything stick 'n up higher than the quarter sized pink granite that made up the entrance way; which for Joe meant just about everything. The rain starts coming down harder but for Joe it is just more of the same trouble he is getting into and he didn't pay it much mind.

Joe stepped up into his cab wet from the rain and threw the thumper towards the passenger seat where it hit, bounces and tears off a piece of the seat. Joe looks skyward, shook his head and says "hmmm" and then grabs his CB mic from its clip. "Hey Bob, come in – over" Joe waited for what he felt is long enough, and yells again loudly into the mic "HEY BOB ARE YOU THERE …"

A scratchy voice echoes back and Joe sounds agitated. Joe waits a minute thinking he is about to get Bob real pissed off… then shaking his head says "LOOK there's some dead guy over here, come down and deal with it - the voice is scratchy and loud but more passive this time. Joe gathers his best calm voice he could mustard up "I said…There's …some …dead …guy …over …at …the …park… entrance, come down… and take care of it …PLEASE… OVER".

There is a long pause of dead air "Bob, you there..." Joe is cut off in mid-sentence by Bob asking if he has hit somebody. Joe came back quickly "Bob…I found this dead guy at the Park entrance", again there is a long pause for which Joe decides he should wait, and after all Bob is sort of his supervisor. But the pause last for a long minute - finally Joe thinks this doesn't sound like the way Bob usually talks. They'd been friends for thirty some years and they both served in Nam together; Joe was just a grunt and Bob was a Sergeant, both had seen some heavy action.

"…Bob, I see this guy… as I was pass'n by the park entrance… I thought he might need some help… over", Joe says slowly…and again there is a long pause. Bob finally came back and told Joe to wait there he would call the sheriff. As Joe turns he hears a thump over by the marker, and quickly looks over at the granite marker - and sees that the corpse has fallen from the perch as the wind picked up. Joe is done with this conversation with Bob and calls 911 on his cell phone.

Joe knew the difference between Bob's idea of the Sherriff and his. There is southern Emerald and then there is northern Emerald where most of the people live. Joe figures that Bob would be calling the main sheriff there in Northern Emerald - and it would be about a two hour wait by the time they processed this whole thing – and with Bob's call in to the sheriff maybe even three hours. Joe began to think about his load and the money he is losing. He feels the time slipping away. Joe passively says, into the CB "…I'm right here - hurry-up, over". Joe took a good look up at the sky and grimaces, it didn't look like it is going to clear…and be just another bad "oh well" day.

Joe thought of the high-minded Northern Emerald people coming down – and pushing their wallets around. Joe hung up the mic on its clip and decided not to respond anymore, things are always hard in Southern Emerald. Joe looks back at the dead man laying on the pink gravel – and thought 'this is shit'. And he pulls his cell phone from his slicker pocket and calls Lee, the sheriff in Barber (southern Emerald); after all he is only maybe 15 minutes away, if that. Beside the Sheriff from Northern Emerald would have to call Lee anyway, but more likely he'd wait and call Lee after he got down here (that is the way it usually is). Joe thought ' …Better to have Lee ask 'n the questions than the Northern Emerald Sheriff…'

Joe punched in Lee's cell number that Lee had given to him – he remembers it right after they found the dead girl in the apartment… Only it isn't her apartment – nobody had lived there in quite sometime – word is a growers had done her in cuz she went to the Feds - and everyone knew the apartment had been used as a grow 'n room. – But the apartment was clean as a whistle no sign of pot, lamps, dirt nothing – and no-one said a word – cept it is a suicide. They never even ask no-body noth'n. Joe grimaces and held the phone tight against his ear – and he could hear the ring,,,,

* * * * *

"Yeah, this is Lee, who is calling?" Lee looks at the caller ID and sees it is Joe – but then Lee never assumes anything. Lee had grown up in southern Emerald, like most back then who came from a logging family. Hard but an honest life – he'd gone to the High School, was the quarterback and was the jock on campus (but never seemed to fit in to the mold everyone thought). His tall stature and strong features made him popular with guys and gals. After High School, he moved on to Emerald State on a football scholarship… but only played one year (said he didn't care for the game anymore). He just couldn't let those Southern Emerald ways go. After he graduated from State, he came back to Barber a few times but was always discourage at the lack of real work – and found that life is changing in southern Emerald in ways that he wasn't comfortable with.

After a while, he left for a spell, like most and married a real pretty girl from High Country County… that he had met while at Emerald State. He moved down to the High Country …where he became Sheriff, raising two boys, But after ten years of marriage his wife left, Lee says, 'never saw it coming'. Lee moved back to southern Emerald where his folks and friends are. Everyone says that High Country had changed him somehow. He is quieter, more a loner …not like he used to be. He never talks about High Country or the girl. There lots of different stories and rumors – but he's a standup guy, even all the big growers said so – and he knew them all from high school. So everyone has left it alone… and gone about their business; now it's just small town talk and whispers.

Lee didn't say much to Joe, just listened and said he'd be right there. Lee's deputy, Donnie, tall and lanky, fresh out of the two year Junior College in the law enforcement program, immediately got up out of the booth that they were sitting in, grabbed his slicker on the side of the booth …and in his haste almost knocks Sally over as she is brings around the coffee.

The Cafe is the local gathering spot, just open for Breakfast and Lunch. 10 booths and a counter with swivel stools – all spaced out nice, so there is no crowding. Marge the owner had decorated the place with cow art and ceramics – they are everywhere. Cows clocks, cow wallpaper, cow salt & pepper shakers …the works. Marge never explains why - she says, she just like the way cows look. Marge had come from the farming area up in northern Emerald but she fit in right anyway – people say she lost her husband and son in some freak farming accident. Marge never talks about it and no one asks.

"…You almost got me there, Donnie…" Sally says with an angelic smile. One of the men at the table says, with an old retired logger's smile, "maybe Donnie is looking for an accidental meeting; after-all she is about the prettiest gal in town…everyone says – lived her whole life right here in Emerald". Everyone at the table gave out a good laugh and turn towards Donnie – who is red faced and fumbling with his slicker.

Sally had started working at the Café when she found out what tending bar is really all about. She was tired of the same old groping she had dealt with before. Donnie just knew that Sally is the kind of girl that he'd never have a chance with in high-school due to his shyness; and he sure didn't want to mess anything up. But there he is again just like in high school, bumping into or knocking something over – and listening to the laughter of the people around him. Donnie stood there embarrassed trying to keep out of everyone's way.

Donnie hastily says, "Let me get that…" but at the same time.

Marge is quietly yelling to Juan, the bus boy "Juan!!" that is all she had to say; Juan always knows what is going on in the Diner, and in town. Juan didn't say anything he just came over with his mop and Donnie's face is redder as he nervously got out of his way.

The Cafe is a small place – you don't need anything big when the town population is only five hundred or so, and everyone knows everybody and their business - usually. Donnie tall and lanky with his flaming red hair, had played basketball up in the Northern Emerald High School and went on to Redwood Tech, the Junior College that offers just about any vocation you would need in Emerald. Donnie is from northern Emerald and only knew a few of the locals. Because he played High School Basketball against the rough and tumble southern Emerald High School, Southern Emerald only had one High School because most of the children were home-schooled. Donnie hadn't managed to fit in the two years he was there. The folks in Southern Emerald respect him – mostly because Lee says he was a good guy; Lee would tell Donnie you just have to give these people some time – Sally is the closest he'd come to getting to know the people of southern Emerald.

Marge never had to say anything very loud or usually more than once. The town folks respect her and have taken her in as one of their own. Marge had come in the town and bought the diner some 7 years back – she never haggled, just paid the Martins what they were asking. The Martins wanted to retire … they 'd owned the diner since before the big '62 flood. Marge took it over and put her own stamp and style on the place, with all her cows and dressed the place up – trying to get some of the tourist trade com 'n through town.

Logging used to be the mainstay of Southern Emerald but with the fall in the price of lumber, jobs were leaving and so were the people. The underground pot industry became the mainstay of southern Emerald.

Emerald is getting noticed by lots of folks and it made some nervous about changes and others that had dollar signs in their eyes or political futures to consider. The growers brought money in and spent most of it in Southern Emerald; but they brought trouble as well; the Government and the potential of Medical Marijuana (what the growers feared the most).

Lee gave his coffee one last sip as he dug into his pocket for some change. From across the table came "I got it Lee". Lee smiled and gave a nod "thanks". A Sherriff didn't make much and especially in an area as poor as Southern Emerald.

Lee could of gone after the County Sheriff's job but he had enough of politics and he had boys to raise. Lots of people owed Lee, but he never ever thought about it – it is just part of the job and he liked the smallness of it all.

Donnie is already out and over talking to Sally as Lee passes him by heading out into the rain. The rain starts to come down harder as Donnie and Lee head for the 4x4 cruiser. Lee decides to drive; …he wants to see how Donnie is going to handle the call. But heaven knows Donnie didn't need more on his mind – Donnie hasn't done so well with the last body that had been found. It isn't that Donnie had any fear of anything – quite the opposite – it is that Donnie tried to do too much and he'd forget to 'look, listen and learn" as Lee had always told him. As Donnie slid into the passenger seat, he tried to catch Lee's eye. Donnie knows it had to be something big because Lee usually never drives. At first, Donnie hated to drive: he felt like it is chauffeuring his boss around but as time went on it felt comfortable and something that he'd gotten used to.

"So what is this all about" Donnie said almost breathless

Donnie hadn't even manage to get his seat belt locked; when Lee started to pull out as if they were just going back to the office four blocks away. Donnie decides to wait as the 'look, learn, listen' tape starts to play in his head. He knew he hadn't done so well with that body that was found face down in the river – that he had missed some things and screwed-up some of the evidence in the case. Lee had never really scolded Donnie about it. He just said, "Always remember to <u>Look</u> at the scene, <u>Listen</u> to what is being said to you and around you and always remember there will be something to <u>Learn</u> (even if you think you have it all put together – there is always something to learn); Look, Listen, Learn."

Donnie sat back to get comfortable as Lee pulled on to the highway exit heading north. "There's a body that has been found" Lee says as the sound of the rain begins to grow louder hitting the windshield. Donnie is trying to contain himself and Lee knew it – so he gave Donnie plenty of time to start his conversation.

"…Who called it in" Donnie responds as he copies Lee's dead pan expression and looks at the rain on the highway through the front windshield of the car.

"Joe" and that is all that Lee responded with, as he thought there may be some hope. But 'that is a pretty good first question - maybe he should lighten up on Donnie just a bit' Lee thought to himself.

"That will make the third body Joe has been involved in finding – this year" Donnie's next question was an irritation to Lee but he just purses his lip and didn't respond. Lee maintains his deadpan expression as they drove the 18 miles to the Park entrance.

As they approach the highway entrance to the Park, Lee responds in a slow calm voice "keep in mind that Joe is a Logging Trucker and there are a lot of places he travels to - at all times of the day". Donnie got it; he knew his statement isn't where Lee wanted to go.

They pull on to the gavel entrance at a slow speed, bouncing through the gravel 'turn-out' and park on the passenger side of Joe's tractor next to the passenger door. Donnie thought that Lee would of park in front of Joe's tractor making any exit by Joe more difficult. 'Look, Listen, Learn' Donnie thought – Joe is not a suspect' Donnie thought – 'don't jump to conclusions'.

Donnie opens the door and waited to see what Lee's next move would be. Lee slowly looks over at Joe's truck, nodded to Joe sitting in it and turns some attention to the passenger truck step then began walking towards the body - just slow enough for Joe to catch-up from the inside of his tractor. Lee can hear Joe slam the cab door shut and hears Joe steps behind him quicken on the gravel as the granite rocks scrapes together under Joe's heavy footsteps. Lee also heard Donnie's shoes against the gravel sounding like he is behind Joe on his right side.

"Donnie, don't forget the tape player, and camera, oh and better get a tape measure also".

Donnie knew that those were all things he should of remember to get 'Look, Listen, Learn' he says to himself. Lee turns to Joe and firmly shook his hand "… not something you want to find on your run back to the mill, huh?" Lee says to Joe in a calm friendly voice. Lee could feel the nervousness in Joe's hand as they shook hands.

Just as suddenly as the hard rain came in – it slowed to a drizzle.

"NO!!...Sorry Lee, its just that times are hard and ...well ...this is going to cost me the day I bet...." Joe's voice shivers in the reply but not just from the cold.

Lee heard the shiver and responded, "Heard from your boy, Frank?"

Joe is somewhat surprised by the question he hadn't heard anything from Lee in months about his son. "Nah, noth'n –talk to him about a month ago, you hear anything?" Joe responds and Lee heard the shiver quiet in Joe's response.

Lee looks straight at Joes eyes and says "No, but I have been asking around." Lee could see from Joe's eyes and manner all Joe wants is to get out and dump off his load. "I thought you said something about the body being up on the Granite ledge?" Lee thought if there is anything... that question ought to do it.

Lee studies Joe's response then quickly yells over at Donnie who had started walking on their right towards the body "...that's a real good spot to start tie 'n with the yellow crime scene tape."

It isn't that Lee thought so much of the area, but calling it a "crime scene" might just slow Donnie a bit. Lee had stopped Donnie just short of the area where the body laid and Donnie is about to step into.

"...Yeah, well he fell off when the heavy wind and rain came in..." Joe came back with a slower response.

"You didn't touch the body...?" Lee asked

Lee could sense something in Joe's voice as Joe looked off to the side where Donnie is tying off the yellow tape.

"I came in from my truck to see..." Joe responds

Lee studies Joe and glances over to Donnie. "...I see he is dead just by the color of his hands... you know you never forget that color once you've seen it" Joe says feeling frustrated that he is going to have to tell the story fifteen or more times to everyone that asked and could feel his load time slipping away.

"... I didn't touch noth'n ...just called it in to Bob...then figured I'd call you before the Eureka boys show's up...". Joe is feeling OK that it is Lee here and he wants to show that he appreciated it. Joe smiles at Lee looking for some recognition.

"That's good" Lee responds but could sense something; "…wouldn't of matter if you did, this place is a mess from all the wind and rain…" Lee looks at Joe closely but with a friendly smile.

"Look"… Joe says "I don't mind sticking round…if ya need me for something."

"You can go on with your load as soon as we are done here, and the Sheriff has checked your statement." Lee quickly responds, as he began to walk slowly towards the body; keeping Donnie in his side view.

Joe turns partially in dismay and starts towards Donnie. Donnie studies what is going on and figures that Joe's statement would be his job and took out his note pad. Watching it turn wet from the drizzling rain and then looked at his writing pen – he had forgot the tape player. Donnie is starting to find it hard to think of many good original questions and tried to picture the 'cheat sheet' that Lee had given him. As Donnie look down at his note pad then looks over to Lee on one knee about two feet from the body. Donnie follows Joe over to his truck and starts to interrogate Joe.

Lee says to Donnie softly "You know you can take better notes in your head and a tape player while you are looking at a man - than if you keep your face down in your notes – that paper looks pretty soaked through…huh?" Lee had hoped that Donnie would get more settled into the business at hand. Donnie finishes with questioning Joe and walks over to Lee.

Lee states, "As for Joe …you got his statement right? And his address…or at least it's in our files somewhere and we can ask about those green logs when we talk and he is calmer" we'll just let him go after the sheriff gets here.

Lee needs Donnie involved in this case; Donnie is feeling embarrassed by Lee's response. "Oh yeah …yeah I just…" Lee cut Donnie off in mid-sentence. "Stand right over there on the right corner of the marker and walk from the marker about 10 feet" Lee says pointing in the direction of the large granite marker.

"You mean over there inside the yellow tape?" Donnie says questioningly. Lee usually has Donnie standing outside the tape to keep bystanders away but

Lee needs Donnie's help with the investigation. Lee is in the yellow taped off area just two feet away from the body, and didn't respond, he just pulls out his telescoping pointer tweezers.

Donnie walks over to the monument corner; "What do you see?" Lee yells over.

Donnie studied the tall ten-foot granite rock marker and the cut out step that had made a mysterious appearance seven feet from the bottom of the marker; the brass plaque three feet off the ground. The brass plaque and map that read the 'Avenue of the Giants National Park' commemorating the park to the Barber town (although the town had little to do with any of it – however the marker included all of the long standing business organizations – all of which had growers on their boards). Donnie knew there is something that he is supposed to see; but it is not like he is looking at the granite rock for the first time. Sally had shown it to him and the step-ups from the back of the rock - on their first date. In bewilderment Donnie couldn't see anything. Donnie turned to Lee and says "Sorry, Lee…" and then he sees it. Donnie motions to the old farmhouse off to the west across the highway and what is left of the green house…Donnie says "strange that you can see the greenhouse fire from here".

Lee didn't say anything right away – he just stood up and looks over at the hillside across the highway from the face of the marker. Lee could just see Derrick's old farm house through the small gap between the mountains some ways off; and just the edge of a greenhouse still smoldering from the fire and one small window on the second level of the house; a large Laurel tree obscured any other part the big old farm house. Then the view was quickly gone blocked by the mountain fog as it moves and lifts through the mountainside.

Lee turns his attention back to Donnie…"why do you say that…" Lee responds with a stern face expression.

"This storms rains and winds came from the north-west and there is a slight rise on front right-side of the Marker step…I never… the body should have been in another position like behind the Marker …" Donnie stops as he sees Lee give him the slightest of nods with a smile; this is a first. And Donnie's heart felt like it would pound through his chest with excitement. In the two years that Donnie has been a deputy with Lee fresh from Redwood College, he has seen that expression but never directed at him.

Lee knelt back down and turns his attention back to the corpse – satisfied with what Donnie had noticed. "… Come over here and give me a hand," Lee says, in a matter of fact voice – hoping not to give Donnie any expectations. Lee looks over the body and he kneels closer to the body he carefully inspects the corpse.

The corpse vest jacket that has blown open and exposes a plant flower in the shirt pocket. He takes out his telescoping metal tweezers. Donnie kneels down and holds his breath, thinking, this is beyond him and wondered what Lee is doing. He looks at Lee's face and sees that look in Lee's eyes. He had seen the concentrated expression on Lee's face before, the girls hanging suicide, the guy they pulled from the river months before, and…Donnie felt he couldn't hold his breath much longer. His knees were beginning to ache as he crouches down further to see if he could see what Lee is looking at.

Donnie could see something it looked like a small purple-reddish flower. It is poking out from the dead mans shirt pocket; just barely exposed under the vest. Donnie thinks that the jacket must have opened up after it fell from the Granite Marker.

Lee reached in under the vest with his long tweezers … "steady …" Lee says to Donnie … in a calm low voice. With Lee's instruction, Donnie held his breath again and Lee's tweezers pull out a flower that Donnie had never seen before. "You can breath now, Donnie" Lee says in the calmest of tone, and Donnie did just that. Lee says, Got an…" Lee began to say.

When Donnie almost automatically pulled out an evidence bag from his rain slicker and covers the pocket. Donnie makes an open tent with his hands around Lee's tweezers so that no water would get into the evidence bag as he opened it.

Lee takes a good sniff of the flower and the bag – "interesting…?" he responds as he raises his finger up to Donnie so that he could smell it also. "I'm going to hazard a guess that the flower comes from an orchid or some plant they use in perfumes" Lee looked up at Donnie with an inquisitive look.

"Well it sure smells pretty, what ever it is..." Donnie responds with a grin. They then finish the examination of the corpse noting the scraps and contusions of the face.

"Donnie <u>NO one</u> … I mean no one!! - Knows anything about this bag, got it…?" Lee says looking straight into Donnie's eyes.

Donnie says automatically "Yes sir".

Lee responds "now go back to the other side of the tape while Lee puts the bag in his rain slicker pocket and snaps it close". Lee walks over to Donnie "How much time we got…?" Lee says as he got up.

Donnie looks at his watch as the beads of rain fell on its surface; "I think we are cutting it close" he responds. Lee looks back towards the hills where he had seen Derrick's farm; then to the right where the highway climbs and takes a big slow left curve – he could see someone's car coming down the highway and thought they'd have about 10 minutes gave or take till the sheriff gets there.

Then Donnie sees it also; the Sheriff SUV vehicle followed by the Corners ambulance but there were two additional black SUVs trailing at a close distance. Donnie says, "who do you think those other two black SUVs are?".

"Feds and investigators I expect" is Lee's short reply. "They've been looking for a reason to get involved down here…that's all" Lee says in just a matter of fact way.

Donnie decides to go ahead and ask, "what is expected" and Lee turns and starts to walk towards the tape. "But won't there be a lot of extra explaining" Donnie is now concerned about Lee's position in all this and the bag that is in his pocket.

Lee knew it is the right question and could hear the concern in Donnie's voice.

They could just start to hear the distant sirens making the approach; and the time is closing in – Lee studies Donnie's eyes "…did you see the blood on Joe's pant leg?" Lee asked pointedly – sure that Donnie hadn't seen it.

"Yes" Donnie replied sheepishly as he was going to bring that up later.

Lee says "well?"

"I got it, Lee sorry" Donnie response.

"…Don't apologize, that is a good question" Lee replied.

"The blood appears to animal probably deer" – that is what Joe says in his statement; Donnie quickly adds "Cause there is no blood anywhere around here and the blood could not of come from the crime scene most likely came from a deer or animal he hit while driving up here. Check underneath his front bumper. You see the blood on the cab step-up right?"

Donnie is sure that is the answer "Joe says he struck a deer near Terryville and that checks with his log records." Donnie explains.

Lee could now hear the sirens of the Sherriff's vehicle sure there is not much more time and no time. Donnie began to quickly respond "and he's got those redwood…."

Just then the Sherriff's vehicle, the ambulance followed by the two black SUVs drove on to the gravel. They didn't seem to pay much respect to the pink granite entranceway as their vehicle came in just a little too fast and dug into the gravel rock as they stopped.

Lee watches as the coroner and his assistant get out of their vehicle first followed by the Northern Emerald Sheriff.

Donnie watches as Lee walked toward the Sherriff; he shook hands with the Sherriff and began a conversation that is out of earshot from Donnie, and the Coroners people just wave as they walk toward the Yellow tape boundary. Donnie is mesmerized by the dance that he perceives is going on.

"See you're doing some investigative training with Donnie"; the Sherriff says hoping he had it right adding, "How is he coming along?"

"He's doing well" Lee says with a pause as he watches two men in suits exit one of the Black SUVs.

"Yeah I figured it is about time…See you brought company" Lee says with a sarcastic smile.

"Yeah you know …just common courtesy – you know how my job gets – besides this is a National Park" the Sherriff responded grimly. They manage a smirk grin at each other. As the two men in suits approach the Sherriff and Lee – Donnie could feel the tension in the air build, as the rain started to letup with only a whisper of a breeze in the air.

Lee yells over toward Donnie to join them; "Donnie you know the Sherriff" Lee says - but Donnie could see the men in suits had hung back as if to wait for the whole group to assemble. Lee says to Donnie "…that about does it you can go now be sure to get the tapes scribed of Joe's statement for the Sheriff as soon as you can".

Embarrassed Donnie says his good byes to the Coroners people, who barely acknowledged him.

"Yes, sir hadn't seen you since…" Donnie says managing an awkward smile. The Sherriff turns to introduce the men in suits and Lee turns with the Sherriff to face their approach. Donnie is nervous and hopes that Lee had some plan.

Just when Lee turns to Donnie and says, "Well schools out I expect you'd like to get back before church starts". Relieved Donnie says his hasty good byes and heads to the cruiser trying not to show his rush to leave.

Donnie looks towards them as he pulls out thinking; Lee and the Sherriff made a formable pair standing shoulder to shoulder as the men in suits approached them.

This is not the first time the granite marker had been used to display a body; in the past it had been a way of the big grower sending a message to the people about keeping their thoughts to themselves. Usually runaways causing problems or people no one knew probably mixed up in something they should not have been doing also. Tweekers (people into meth making it and selling it), type of people no on wants around. But this is different the clothes are new, the body appears to be someone of money

CHAPTER 4
QUANTEX/HOOLIGANS

The Dallas morning October sun hit hard against the tall glass office buildings as it broke through the horizon; and the manicured dark green landscaping seems to drink in its glare. Ed pulls into his reserve parking spot in front of the building. He sits quietly and studies the shadows of the newly planted trees gathering his thoughts for the day. Ed is not one to jump instantly into anything. He exits his car and takes a short glance at his reflection in the driver side window.

Mr. GQ they call him and that is just fine with Ed except for the sarcastic comments about his age; young Turks don't know any better. As Ed approaches the Quantex ultra modern, all glass seventeen story office building, the security guard quickly opens the large glass door.

Ed immediately gives his always-friendly corporate smile and says, "Thank you, and Good Morning".

The security guard greets Ed with "Good morning Sir". Ed smiles as usual as he signed in and the security guard hands him the Wall Street Journal. "They say we're going to get some rain, sir" the security guard replied with a smile.

Ed returned the smile "Well we could sure could use it; thanks, I'll be sure to have my umbrella handy".

"Yes sir" the security guard says in an automatic reply.

PURPLE

To those who didn't know Ed, he has the appearance of one of those ultra intimidating executive types. Ed is an older man who loved his age, tall lanky (6' 5") frame always allowed him a quicker pace; he walked with that straight upright posture and long stride, wearing impeccable suits, that are the latest in business wear with his usual impeccable Windsor knotted tie that all the younger execs will be copying in the coming weeks.

However, no matter how reserved and polished he looks, his smile could light up a room or a secretary's heart; and that is the Ed that most people knew. Ed is the consummate salesman – always quick with a joke or story but equally quick to make sure that everyone is engaged in whatever the conversation that is going on. Ed enjoys playing the part of the Executive Vice President, he has worked hard to get where he wants to be and at 64 he is still ready to take on the "young Turks"; or to help an older woman remember how young she is. Ed is definitely a ladies man, all the young secretaries could vouch for that; a man well respected, a man's man a person who people would listen to – even his non-corporate friends and acquaintances.

As Ed pushes the elevator button he turns back to the guard and with a smile ask; "has our young Mr. Swartz checked in"?

"Oh yes sir, about 20 minutes ago" the guard says returning the smile.

Ed already knows that Michael Swartz is in – after seeing his car in the parking lot; it is just that Ed didn't like empty air; that place where you feel something needed to be said to fill the silent spaces. Ed is already in the ultra-modern mirror and veneered wood elevator when the guard responds; and as usual it is empty this time of the morning. Ed inserts his pass card key for the top floor.

As the elevator opens to the tile entry at the top floor, Ed sees that not all the lights are on and turns the corner, flipping on the remaining light switches. There were only a small handful of people that could manage the hours it takes to stay 'on your game' as Ed called it. Ed always paces himself and became use to the rigors of the corporate life and job; client golf (which he is not particularly good at) promoting Quantex, sales and Ed's passion the creation of new business products. Ed is known for his promotion of new products, people and ventures; and now he thinks he has an idea that will revolutionize Quantex in the Pharmaceutical business.

Ed could see Michael's office lights on down the hall; and he turns back to his own office, crossing the open space Berber carpet to the corner of the building; closing the large Mahogany office doors. Ed always needs time these days to get his day straight and his head ready for the fray of the games – deciding where he will have room for his social agendas.

'Must keep the troops happy' Ed thinks out loud – of course how to get interest going in "his Projects". Not to mention Ed's love of his office panoramic view, that also overlooked the picnic style patio three floors below; yes. That is quite a view during the summer ... Ed smiled and strolled to his desk thinking he will be glad when summer is back and the girls will be eating lunch on the grass maybe even sun bathing.

Ed sat down in his modestly style high back leather desk chair, designed more for his back but stylishly decorated to suit the office. As Ed spread the W S Journal across his desk - more a showpiece for him – people thought all top executives read it – so... There is a knock on the door. As it opened (there were very few people that would automatically walk into Ed's office unannounced). Ed is expecting it.

"Good Morning Ed, I just want to catch you before the morning gets started" Michael says, knowing that he is one those privileged few that could walk in unannounced.

Ed gave his usual very friendly smile and replied, "Just give me a few seconds". Michael patiently stood and watches as Ed finish laying out the WSJ and took out a red pointed highlighter and began scanning and circling a few columns as he turned the pages.

"There's a good one on page eight, 'Quantex explorer'", Michael says directing him to the section and Ed immediately turned the page to it and highlights the title.

Ed quickly scans the small article and gave one of his "hmmm" grins "Don't tell me you've been found out," Ed says as he glances over the article. "Oh this is about Tom Harding's group, this is not exactly news", Ed responds.

"Next to last paragraph, 'Alternative medical….' Michael knows that Ed could read it faster than he could tell him about it.

"Thanks"; Ed response raising his eyebrow to Michael; "…but I want to hear about your trip" Ed says getting up and pointing to the stylish yet comfortable leather couch on the other side of the office.

Ed is the consummate cordial host and liked the business casualness - that helped to make people at ease. Although Michael and Ed are well past that stage, Ed had taken Michael under his wing when Michael was stuck as an Assistant Vice President of Research and Development; Ed was afraid that Michael was going to leave for 'Greener pastures' feeling stuck in a glass ceiling. Michael is one of the rising 'young Turks' and just knows he was stuck and needs some other challenges. Ed and Michael (Michael to his friends) had become friend's not just business associates. In the office, people are always surprised that they seem fit for each other. Michael with his short 5' 6" stature – rushing here and there - with that rumbled look – even when he has on a new suit. Michael, following Ed's lead where appropriate always deferring to his boss, as Edward. At the local clubs when telling jokes they were always at the ready to finish each other's sentences.

As they sit down Ed asks "So was Amsterdam all that you thought it would be" trying to make sure that his agenda is set with Michael – before Michael brought up his agenda.

"That's what I came to talk to you about" Michael knew to pay attention to Ed's first few sentences that they would be Ed's public 'tell'; and Michael would always take the lead when he felt it is his turn – waiting for the slightest of pauses or a raised eye brow from Ed.

"Amsterdam is all you said it would be" Michael starts with a smile in his voice "but I have to tell you about the competition";

Ed interrupts to put Michael back on track "…let's talk about that later this evening over at Hooligan's, …now tell me you got enough rest and about the girls".

Michael took the lead and they talked awhile until Helen knocks on the door opening it ever so slightly. "…Do you have your coffee, Mr. Falconer" Helen says with a familiar tone as she walks across the room and adjusts the window blinds. Helen had been with Ed since Ed's Assistant VP days – long hours and many a private discussions - work and personal. Helen always made sure she had the latest in office and personal gossip for Ed; and that she had blocked off any potential embarrassing consequences for him, or at least made him aware of them.

"Helen, you see that WS Journal piece – Michael pointed out to me" Ed says to Helen always making sure that people got credit where credit is deserved.

"Didn't I say to look out for Tom" Helen responded quickly, continuing, "Tom has no idea how I work to keep these Young Turk's inline, you know that".

"But still the WSJ" Ed says as his hand moved in a big expanse.

Helen just gave a smirk to Ed and replied "So I'll assume you are set for the morning, Good Morning to you Mr. Swartz" Ed had taught Helen well, pay attention to everyone 'you never know, who would be where, next'.

"Good Morning Helen" Michael says as he rose to leave.

"Don't go on my account; its only me" Helen quips. Michael smiles knowing that it is the secretary that 'makes the man' and responds; "catch-up with you later, I have to go and 'entertain' the troops".

✳ ✳ ✳ ✳ ✳

The business day slipped away as it usually did – some crises here or there; business fires to be put out – just all in the normal day of ringing office telephones and cell-phones – with closed door meeting or something other. However, Michael spent the day lost in daydreams of Amsterdam and the incredible adventure he had there. His daydreams are interrupted from time to time through out the day by the all to constant duties of 'the job'. He feels certain that he should have taken a day or so before coming back to work; but then - would he come back - he thought.

Michael smiled and began to realize that he is still high from the new weed he had found. He felt quite sure that Ed and he were going to have some real fun making a lot of money – and that he to could afford a 40' sail boat. Oh he is high all right – he thought – but it is more than the weed; for the first time he thought he could really do something – make a difference. He began to think that this weed is more than just weed – that it had properties that were more than just THC – (Tetrahydrocannabinol is the principal psychoactive constituent of cannabis/marijuana).

He could feel his thoughts. He feels the urge to take some of it to his friend at the Quantex lab for testing; but that might be over-stepping and he owes ED quite a lot. He had to get back to Derrick; that would be his recommendation to Ed. Oh Ed probably has that bit worked out – but he has an in with Derrick. After their meeting in Amsterdam; oh that was magical….

Ed knocked on Michael's door – which is open, just a crack to catch the all the sounds of "business"; and it brought his head and mind back into perspective – for which Ed gave him a smile.

Ed says "Hooligan's…?" with a raised eyebrow – Michael is expecting Ed but made sure not to show it; better to have your boss ask you – than others, or for you to ask your boss … – Ed had taught him.

"I'm right behind you …" Michael responds with a grin. Michael sat there a few more moments and reminds himself that this is the "real" work. Michael neatened up his desk and locked away his notes – he needs them for later. Michael opened the closet – Ed had talked him into this office because it had a closet – of all things – and of course is in the middle of what is going on – Ed's eyes and ear – and he felt useful in that role - for now anyway. From his locked desk drawer he pulled out the bag of his "samples" that he had made up for Ed the night before. He stuffed a smaller baggy in his pants pocket and the rest in his brief case; he thought maybe he would try some on the way over. Derrick had tried to explain how this is more than THC and Michael is beginning to understand – he smiles – 'yep still high' he thought to himself. A small 'toot' would be good for the drive. He closes his briefcase and pats his pants pocket with a smile; grabs his coat and locks up.

✻ ✻ ✻ ✻ ✻

The evening bar scene at Hooligan's is filled with the usual crowd; but this is Ed's place – a place to feel comfortable and Michael is beginning to understand why Ed likes it.

You have to be practically from Ireland to get any service, or a regular to get great service or be introduced by someone; as Michael had been. Ed insists on calling Michael, Michael, because it sounds more Irish even though as everyone knows he is Jewish and from New York – but he is with Ed and that is all that matters.

The bar is a long Cherry wood Bar with a granite marble top; brass railing for your feet – and has the man's bar look, the bar stools are beginning to show some wear on the leather seat – but no matter – and the marble floor always looked like it is well used – that shows even in the dim light. There is every liquor you could imagine placed carefully in front of the mirror and cut glass wall behind the bar – and if it weren't there – it would be there the next day (if you were a regular) it is the Hooligan's style. The Tiffany style booth lighting with the frosted glass over-hanging lights from the ceiling dimly soft lit.

The front bar booths were high backed style with green leather seating – they seem to always be in the best condition – not the Same could be said for the booths toward the back. As Ed says - if you want a discussion … to sit there (pointing to the booth) – no one really used them unless they did want to be there; many a night Ed had proved it is just the place to do real business.

Not many of the people from Quantex ever made it there – and that suits Ed just fine; but everyone at Quantex knew it is Ed's place. Oh a few of the office 'young Turks' had tried to invade Ed's space a time or two in the bar, until the wrong beer is served or a drink is 'accidentally' spilled. Hooligan's took care of their own and always made sure that Ed is taken care of, even when he has a few to many, which is at times too often. Ed and Michael make there way through the crowd and noise, with the normal Irish greeting and smiles. Hooligans' is in the city and often not suited for the office or the suburbanites – it had the appearance of a 'very classy dive' as Ed calls it.

Ed and Michael make their way to the rear back end of the bar – where there are usually good "let me alone" stools to be had.

"Now tell me about the competition" Ed says keeping his voice low.

"Mr. Falconer, that table to-wards that back is available" the waitress smiles.

Ed nods appreciatively, at Hooligan's bar tender - they knew when Ed's voice is low it meant he needed a quiet space. Ed throws down a ten on the bar and nods to the bartender, it is more than he should but then that is Ed. Ed motions to the waitress for another round of "neat" Scotch and a soda back, the waitress knew the right 18 year old Scotch that is under the counter is what Ed is after she'd have to watch 'em. This is going to be serious business she thought with a smile.

The table in the back is dim light as if made for something private and Hooligan's usually had their tableware on the table so no one would sit there. You could always hear the kitchen. Ed used to say its there to drown out the real conversations. All the tables, and the booths, are made with dark hard wood – the booths are 'high back' – you never knew who is there until you come upon the table.

Ed and Michael deposit their expensive suit coats on the booth side brass hook. Michael is feeling high from the drive over but excited to tell Ed of the adventure. "It is just as you say; it is …just wow…every kind of 'weed and apparatus ' you could imagine from all over the world; and the 'special proprietor reserves stuff is, as you say, 'to be taken very seriously'. The West Coast is represented mostly by Emerald County, big growers, and some from small growers with potential. But there is stuff from all over; and I did see a couple of major players represented – Derrick Taylor and Paul Dunn. Ed shrugged his shoulder and gave his head a slight shake of non-recognition. Ed listens as Michael described the Amsterdam Marijuana convention's almost carnival like atmosphere of the Cup competitions and all the surprising varieties of marijuana, paraphernalia and people – oh yeah the people. A large smile took over Michael's conversation; Ed could see that he had chosen well and Ed lifted his glass to Michael in a salute.

Ed did know Derrick from his AVP days,when Ed was one of the young 'Turks' working his way up through the corporate ladder; but he didn't want to do anything that would take away from Michael's moment

"… But this Derrick guy is…a major player in California in 'the Cup' Michael continued…and as the evening wore on Ed began to see that Michael's Scotch is beginning to show – as Michael began to slur. "…And these two guys – I guess it is this Paul guy - had a group of major players around them; all talking yields, grow space, sodium light concentrations, fertilizer ratio, water needs, inside vs. outside growing…" Michael is getting very caught up in the telling of his adventure.

As Ed sits there he found himself drifting more away from Michael's conversation about Derrick; after all it's why Ed had chosen to send him there… to see if the rumors of maximum THC were true. The waitress briefly interrupts their conversation to bring another round that Ed has ordered. It is the moment Ed needed to get into Michael's excitement – to the depth of it – find out if he had any 'product'. "So you met these guys…?" Ed says breaking into Michael's conversation before Michael starts up again.

"Yeah…" Michael quickly responds; and Ed's heart leaps… it is exactly what he expects of Michael. Michael took a large gulp of the Scotch he ordered. Ed sees that he needs to cut to the chase with Michael before Michael begins to swim in his own story. Ed looks at Michael and in just above a whisper says "Product…?" Ed hopes that Michael would bring the volume of his conversation down and copy the whisper tone that he is using.

"Huh…?" Michael looking glassy eye and puzzled Michael thinks product…? " THE PRODUCT…!! …"OH YEAH…!!" Michael blurts out causing people nearby at the bar to turn and look at Michael as if his voice is out of tune with the bar and he had disturbed them. Ed quickly put a firm grip on Michaels forearm as Michael is raising his glass of Scotch off the table for another gulp. Michael's grip on his Scotch is less secure and half the drink spills on the table; dripping down on to Michael's trousers. Michael instantly knew what he has done – breaking Ed's golden rule 'never show', but he draws more attention as he suddenly stood up…almost falling back into the booth. "Sorry…boss; guess I got carried away".

Ed stands up with him, grabs the glass of soda he ordered and took Michael's arm ushering Michael toward the back hall restroom just around the corner from them. As they entered the checker tile restroom – that is more suited for the kitchen - Ed takes a quick survey under the toilet stalls to see if they are alone. Ed pulls out a few paper towels and pour the soda on them over the white porcelain sinks; "You obviously got some product and used it …and didn't wait to share it!!", Ed says with a half chuckle half serious tone; as he hands Michael the soda soaked paper towels and dry ones.

Michael stands trying to get his bearings and realizes maybe that extra 'toot' in the car was a bad idea – but he chuckles anyway.

Michael gives Ed a look of 'Oh Shit' but not over the spilled drink. "You say 'the' product not 'their' product" as he pats his trouser with the dry towels.

"The' – product – 'their' product what is the difference? The main thing is that you have it" Ed says as he turns and pulls more paper towels from the white metal dispenser.

Michael leans back against the sink cabinet "…how did you know…?" Michael says as he clumsily tries to rub out the drink that had spilled on his trousers.

"Know what…?" Ed quickly responded only half looking at Michael "Well… of course… I knew…or …actually hope that at least there would be some people and …'the product' available. There are rumors that there is pot floating around in the world from Emerald County that has an unbelievable amount of THC in it. And I thought rather than …beat the …

Michael cut Ed short, with "…beating the bushes for it …you send me to where the product is being distributed and sold by.". Michael turns and faces the mirror not knowing whether to laugh or just what to do… Michael reached into his suit pants pocket and pulls out a clear plastic baggie with a small purple-brown wrapped ball looking object in it. Handing the object to Ed he says "…. is this what you had in mind" and gives Ed a wily smile.

After-all, Amsterdam had been more fun than when Ed sent him to Yemen and Ed had to go recue him from that Nomad group – that had kidnapped him.

Ed studies the packet and quickly put it in his suit pocket; and then gives Michael a stern look, saying, "Look Michael… you are the best field man I have… but at times you get too focused on the task and not in the enjoyment of the of the adventure…you know the journey. Relax, you'll live longer… Do you know what the next plan is? We got to find Derrick?" Ed finishes "then tomorrow morning you catch a flight to this Derrick I'll cover for you" Ed says sternly and studied Michael's face for warning signs… the last thing he needs now is a scene in a restroom pub.

Michael turns and just shakes his head and says, "…point well taken…but you could of given me some kind of hint why I am there; any… way you have what you are after".

Ed gives Michael a smirk and raises his eyebrow. "Why don't you stay here and I'll get the check then we'll head out the back to give this a try…" Ed doesn't wait for Michael response, and casually walks out to take care of the check.

Ed walks over to the back of the bar where they had been – and pats the man on the shoulder that is sitting on the stool – "Please see that the Bar-tender gets this – tell him it's from Ed", and he lays a hundred dollar bill on the bar.

Ed is trying to return to the men's room when the bartender says "Hey Ed… should we of carded the young lad?" and everyone near them at the bar laughs.

Ed feels that to rush off will be bad manners and pulls out a James Madison dollar coin from his jacket pocket flicks it in the air caught it and slapped it down on the bar.

"Tails Ed – you'll not be getting a free one this time" the bar tender says with a shout and put his hand palm down on top of Ed's and says "I hear that some people can turn a coin from one side or the other…while the coin is under their palm…".

Ed laughs as he takes his hand away

"Heads…", the crowd shouts and Ed tosses the coin to the waitress and says this should cover it. The waitress smiles and tosses it to the bartender"; a new James Madison Ed, you shouldn't of …" all the regulars at the pub knew Bartender's passion for collecting silver dollars". I was just looking for a reason to give it to ya" Ed says in his best Irish brogue… and the people at the bar laughed; but the bartender knew the coin is worth more than the tab and stuck it in his pocket.

Ed pats his pocket – feeling the bump, of the packet Michael had given him;

and gave a wave as he quickly walked back toward the restroom, but when Ed entered the Men's Room he didn't see Michael anywhere.

A man that is entering one of the stalls says, "I think your friend has had enough and left through the back kitchen door" the man chuckling as he closes the stall door.

Ed quickly walks through the kitchen and out on to the dark poorly lit alleyway, but Michael is gone. Ed thinks he must of gotten light headed and needed some air.

The alley smells of places businessmen should not be after dark - Ed took out his cell phone and quickly calls – but there is no answer and his call went straight into a message mailbox. Ed looks about as he walks hurriedly down the alleyway, calling again on his cell phone again and then again, hoping that he would or wouldn't see Michael collapsed in the alley. Ed is pissed and visibly upset pursing his lips and cursing to himself; he thought that's all I need is a drunken employee walking around with … Ed thought "…Oh shit what if he has another package in his jacket or car…it would be just like that son-of-a-bitch…" Ed says just under his breath while glancing around. As he again pats the packet of his suit pocket feeling slightly bad that he'd deceived his friend … but then chuckles. Ed thinks to himself at how quickly Michael had put all the pieces together. Ed knows that Michael is quick and that just maybe Michael did learn something after all, in that Yemen fiasco. Ed tries Michael's cell phone…again.

CHAPTER 5

PRODUCT

Michael needs some air and walks passed the alley up the darken sidewalk. He hates the city's side streets as they always made him nervous. 'But that is where Ed's hangouts are he thinks to himself. "Now if he could just remember where he has parked his car," he mumbles to himself as he crosses the street. The area smelled of urine and fresh garbage that had just been taken out, and he thought 'I better try to retrace my steps I guess I'm turned around'.

Michael re-crosses the street when he sees two men he thought he'd remembered from the bar and gave the best smile he could manage.

"Are you with E's...Ed friend from Hooligan's?" The man says, as they were passing side-by-side.

Michael looks at man's rumpled suit that needs to be re-fitted and his retail tie with polished shoes and thought 'well at least he has on a tie. "Yeah?" Michael isn't real sure if they were friend or foe – with rumpled suits, but nice shoes. Michael says "I got turned around perhaps you could point me …."

One of the heavier set gentleman replies "…buddy you shouldn't be driving. We can take you back to the pub – Ed is probably still in there drinking people under the bar".

Well if nothing else... they certainly knew Ed, maybe? ...Well, and he shouldn't be driving; Michael thought to himself. "Sure…" as best that Michael could slur out – Michael could stand up to the best of them when it came to alcohol but something seems wrong about the way that he felt.

He has taken a 'toot' of the weed but it is as if he knew and could figure things out – like his mind is in over-drive - but he is obviously drunk. The three of them head on across the street towards the two men's car.

As they enter the parking garage elevator the heavyset man says, "…so you got any of that 'PRODUCT'… that you can share?".

Michael thinks 'OH SHIT' they must of heard the conversation and his outburst of 'PRODUCT"; and could sense immediately that he is in danger as the men entered the elevator; Michael put out his arm and stopped the elevator door. The heavyset man turns and grabs Michael's suit sleeve; Michael spun to one side letting the jacket go. He quickly ran out into the parking lot and the up the stairs and heard "…you got nowhere to run to kid - we just want the PRODUCT".

Michael screams "ED" as loud as he can, as he hit the second floor step, but he thought no one could hear him in the stairway and his damn cell phone is in my jacket pocket.

Michael hears the second floor elevator door open and one of the men say "you get the stairway just don't do anything stupid".

Michael hears the footsteps pounding the concrete stair steps. He jumps to the first floor landing and could hear the footsteps closing; 'just my luck I got an over-weight track guy after me' he thought. Michael pulls open the exit door and could hear tires squeal as they rounded the corners inside the parking garage. Michael could feel the heaviness of his legs 'damn waste of good scotch' as Michael threw-up and kept running down the street. He notices some people walking the along opposite side of sidewalk and he yelled "…call 911… I'm Michael…" his voice is cut short as he heard tires squealing and turning onto the street. Michael heads down a back passageway thinking '…thank goodness for small alleyways.'

The passage led him to the back of what appeared to be a collection of dumpsters; he could see the car lights reflect against the far brick building of the alley leading to the dumpsters. He quickly shoves two of the dumpsters together to block the alley and runs as fast as he can back down the passageway. He begins yelling "call 911" looking back over his shoulder and runs into the people that he had seen across the street.

"Hey man - what the fuck…" comes from the passerby Michael falls as he knocks down someone;

"Hey call the cops…?" the one guy says to him "…sure…but you going to owe me for mess'n up my jacket…" came from the other man, as he is getting up.

Michael could hear a siren in the distance and could feel his heart pounding as sweat poured down on his face. Michael reaches into his pant's pocket and pulled out the baggie he had been carrying and slapped the baggie into the hand of the man that is standing; "here, it's yours, some great shit"

The other man getting up says "…what the fuck…man, you go'n get us busted?". Michael pulled out his wallet and emptied the bills into the man's hand "…you better not… be no cop".

Michael could hardly breath as he sees the police car round the street corner, and just shook his head… managing to say "…no", "…take …it".

"This better be ok," the one person says as the police car pulls in facing the sidewalk.

The officers quickly and aggressively exit their vehicle staying behind their car doors; Michael quickly throws his hands up "…yelling I'm Michael and I asked these guys to called 911 for me" and then Michael dropped to his knee being supported by one of the men. Michael says, "I am coming from Hooligans and someone tried to rob me" the police officer walks him over to the curb and tells him to sit and to show some identification. Michael gives them his driver license and says I am trying to get to the airport I have a plane to catch. Michael goes on to explain he "went to the bar with a friend and needed some air so I walked out and got turned around.

The cops ask for the "friends" name –

Michael responses "Ed Falconer he is my boss" the cops tell him they know

Ed from Hooligans he has been very generous with the Policeman Association. Michael breathes a sigh of relief. The police tell him that he will not be able to get on a plane but that they can take him back to Hooligans or to a hotel. Michael opts for the hotel.

✳ ✳ ✳ ✳ ✳

The next morning Michael awakes full of energy – which he finds hard to believe given the night before. He pays his hotel bill and catches a cab to the airport. Once in the airport he is obsessed with looking over his shoulder but he navigates the airport crowd well other than finding it much too entertaining for words. The flash of colors and the noises seem to paint more color in his head – and he realizes that he is still tripping – 'but how could this be' his paranoia runs through his mind like a freight train he knows now he is still tripping and smiles. He quickly goes to an airport ticket terminal and he manages to check through security and is aware that he has no baggage but manages to pass through the scanner. He examines his ticket and thinks oh my god I have a window seat – I can play tourist and look at the scenery; heaven knows I don't want to try any conversation.

The trip is uneventful with no conversation, no kids to deal with just the bumpy air; its all good. He manages to exit the plane easily taking his time; and the smiles not too much. The SFO large International airport is larger than he remembers but it is fairly uneventful, except for the constant looking over his shoulder; and the stares at his rumpled look. As he walks down the exit ramp from the airplane he found that he could not shake the feeling of being followed; and his anxiety increases as he entered the deplaning waiting area.

He walks down the corridor past gate 64, 62, and halfway down the passage way he casually walks over to gate 60 and sits in one of the waiting benches facing the direction he had come from. He noticed that gate 60 is a delayed flight leaving for Denver; he chose a seat facing the passengers deplaning from his flight and others…just in case his fears are real – might as well face it head on. He grabs a newspaper from the seat next to him and places it as if reading it so that his face is mostly covered. He glances at the passengers as they pass by, and thought to himself, there is a reason that he is Ed's best field agent – caution – always caution – then he chuckles to himself as he remembered Ed saying "You have to enjoy the journey…enjoy the journey yeah, right!"

Now, getting a hold of Ed is his highest priority, he is sure that Ed would start to worry, because he is always early - even on the worst of late nights: but Ed did tell him to find Derrick as quickly as he can. And now it is early morning; he glances around and sees the Internet booths on the other side of the aisle, and quickly makes his way over there. Michael logged into the computer using the airport connection, feeling fairly secure after his scan of the exiting passengers; however he found his security tested as empty seats around him began to fill. Michael nods at the man that has just sat down next to him "finally, getting out of here, huh" he says. The man nodded and continued to read his computer screen.

Michael quickly logged on to his remote connection at the Quantex desktop and accesses his mail account; and typed in 'It's a good time to enjoy the sun – I'll work from here things are humming along' and hits send to Ed and Helen. He feels fairly sure that they would let Ed know and that he would figure it out.

As Michael shutdown his computer connection he notices that the man sitting next to him has left and then sees that there were further delays for the Denver flight; and feels relieved. Michael feels fairly confident that he has not been followed as he rose from his seat and headed further down the exit aisle toward the car rental stands. However, he looked at his suit pants, rumpled, and thought that the morning flight hadn't help, nor the cab rides; OR… the stay at the Hotel. He is fairly sure that the police bought his story about nearly being mugged, that he had drinks with friends. Imagine Ed's gift to the Police Association paid off and he would have to remember that in the story he had to tell Ed.

Michael hurries down the corridor of busy people to the bus taking the people to the rental car agencies. He has taken this same trip from many other airports – but for the first time he noticed the preoccupation of everyone with the day's business. All rushing about - stressed …and trying to appear that they weren't … and every once in while the terrified "newbie's" hoping that someone would tell them what they had to do – or the overly confident ones making idle chit-chat with just about anyone – yes they were all here – trying desperately not to notice …or be noticed.

The rental car agent barely took notice of his rumpled look or the lack of a briefcase or luggage. He thought 'Rush hour is certainly the time – to be invisible and not to be noticed'. Michael smiles at the agent when he ordered the same type of rental car that all the people seem to be ordering – he thought 'I fit right in, without fitting in'. He didn't ask for directions for fear of the attention – but grabbed the desk sheet map and walked to the rental car and simply drove away – laughing to himself that he had never noticed how invisible he was.

As he drove his rental car – which is an upgrade from the small size rental he requested – he drove on to the highway in the morning rush of traffic - and headed across the Golden Gate Bridge that would take him up the long stretch of Highway and on to Emerald. He began to plan out his day; and looks for a place to have breakfast, listening to his grumbling stomach and wondering if this is the best way to Emerald '…. Oh yeah I need a map', the one he has, has no detail, he mumbled to himself – 'well at least I'm not looking over my shoulder' he thought - as he looked in the rear-view mirror.

Crossing the bridge led him into a suburban town – which appeared to him to be a large bedroom community. Following the rental car sheet map he followed the highway into the town of Novato. He stopped for some breakfast. No one seemed to mind his rumpled appearance and he see's they had maps of the area, which cover the rest of the state.

The café appears to be friendly enough as he is enjoying the meal at the counter he could see a familiar car pull in to the café. He remembers seeing it only because the man that rented it was standing behind him in line at the rental agency. He thinks this paranoia has to stop – but when he sees the man get a package take out breakfast, he jumps at the chance, and has the waitress wrap-up his meal in a take out bag. As he pulls back on to the highway he didn't notice the car anymore – and tried to settle himself down.

As he heads up the highway, a cool mist begins to fill the air. The countryside seems to begin to change into a softer mellower atmosphere – with soft rolling hills, tall pine trees and small artsy shops – he had expected for the tourist trade.

Derrick had told him about going to a University on the Bay near the city – and how driving up this Highway, is the only way to reach Emerald. The highway would change from a rush like mad city – then a casual atmosphere, and the art shops would appear – and after a longer stretch of driving he would climb into the Redwoods. Michael wonders how it might have changed since Derrick first drove north to Emerald. The concentration of people that filled its corridors he guesses would be the largest impact – but that is to be expected anywhere especially in an area so inviting.

Michael imagines that it is quite different back in the '60's Summer of Love' when Derrick told him he first went to Emerald.

Michael settles into the drive northward much pass San Francisco and remembers after he came back from Amsterdam he discovers who Derrick and Paul are that he had heard so much talk about (although he never really met Paul). He has been curious why they drew such attention as if they were the Grower's growers of marijuana. The two of them seemed to be treated like a major - major players; and they always seem to have people around like some kind of security. Michael had guessed it is to make sure that the 'riffraff' didn't' bother them; the drinks and foods were always served to meet their needs. However, Michael senses that they did not enjoy the attention; or at least Derrick did not – and Paul seemed to vanish or as Derrick told him once "he just didn't like crowds".

He remembers the judging at the convention and how obvious it is that you had to know the score of what is going on. Michael smiles at the memory of one evening after the Big Marijuana judging from all over the world. Michael happened to meet Derrick at this out-of-way bar – which Michael found and enjoyed.

Derrick was sitting in the back of the dark corner when he enters the bar – a 'dive' if ever there is one – not decorated anyway in particular – but he did see lots of Emerald and general marijuana posters mixed in with the psychedelic ones. Derrick seemed to be people watching and slightly amused at something or other. Michael didn't see anyone about so he took a chance and approached

Derrick; and this burly man blocks his way just as he is about to say something to Derrick. Derrick quickly dismissed the burly man – with a jester "… I told you guys to stop that shit" and shook his head. "If he wants to sit…then let him sit…damn". Derrick says and starts to get up to leave; obviously irritated at the attention.

Michael sees a fleeting chance "I was about to order a Cognac …can I offer you one … or is that against the rules" as he says with a chuckle. Michael noticed that Derrick had been drinking chilled Vodka from one of those tall Russian type double shot glasses.

Derrick gave Michael a glancing look "…are you for real or just trying to talk with me or bribe me?"

"Neither I am in sales for a company call Quantex you may have of heard of us" Michael is trying to appear in his best upper management persona that he could muster …a copy of Ed he hopes.

Derrick spewed his drink that he was about to finish and laughs, "…Sit - sit…this I got to hear. Hello I am Derrick; I almost worked for you guys; you guys have really turned the agriculture world upside down" Derrick says with a straight-laced look at Michael.

"Two of your best Cognacs", Michael says quietly to the bartender.

" You know the best is Louie XIII" Derrick says quietly to Michael"; why don't you get something that will draw less attention…" Derrick yells over at the bartender "…give us some of that Hine that we were drinking last night…. it's on your expense account…right?" Derrick says with a smirk. And then he introduces himself and they shake hands.

Derrick's seems to have farmer's hands – a firm grip and hands of calluses. "You know I remember you from yesterday - that was a closed private judging… did you know? …But I guess you know how to get in where you want to go?" Derrick says with a smile but a curiosity look.

The bartender says, "there you go – it's $45 a glass so drink up";

Michael quickly responds by giving the bartender his credit card "…run a tab for me; if you please". Michael turned back to Derrick and raised his glass "…

to Amsterdam" and they took a sip of the amber liquid. "So what makes you so popular; if you don't mind me asking?" Michael says as if he is meeting a new friend.

Derrick smiles and responds, - "let's not talk shop!".

"How do you mean?" Michael asks with a straight face, thinking he certainly did not want to offend, a new friend.

Derrick turned back to his glass "Ok…why are you here, you were here watching the judging of our amateur weed competition last night…?"

Michael decided that it is best to come clean and explain, "I have no idea. My boss sent me here to sample the product to see if there is some 'extra heavy' product on the market". Derrick looked on as Michael explained what he did and that he really had no idea why he was there.

Derrick is cautious but is enjoying Michael's company as the night wore on. Then after their third Hine, Michael sees Derrick pull a small baggy from his jacket pocket, laid it on the table pushing it toward Michael. "I have to go soon, you can enjoy it in good spirit. This may be what you were looking for – and if you are ever up my way stop by…I live in the Redwoods of Emerald near the town of Barber at least that is the closest town" Derrick responds in a very friendly sort of fashion. He shakes Michael's hand as if this had been a beginning friendship or at least a connection of sorts.

Michael took the baggy and opened it cautiously expecting the normal musty sweet smell of marijuana; but it is more – much more than he had expected. The smell is somehow deeper, sweeter, and richer, with purple leaves and a smell filled with…Michael found he pulling back a bit – it must be the Cognac, he thought. Michael urged Derrick to stay for another.

Michael put the gift into his jacket pocket and looked over at Derrick who now had a smirk on his face. "Nice aroma…huh?" Derrick says looking at Michael's surprise expression. "This stuff will blow your mind forget all the acid trips and all the Sativa grass you've tried. This stuff is the real deal it will send you into yourself… and be careful a little bit goes along way. Derrick felt at ease and stayed seeming to have feelings that a friendship is developing.

Michael relaxes and asks Derrick about how he got into growing. Derrick explains how he stumbled into becoming a pot grower and his experimentation with strains of marijuana.

Derrick weaves his story of how in '67 when Derrick, Paul along with a girl, Sarah, had taken off to Emerald at Sarah's urging. The University studies and Graduation were over, Derrick is walking out with a degree in Biochemistry, Paul with a degree in Botany and Sarah with her Art & Education degree. "Sarah as her friends called her" Derrick says with a chuckle. Paul had a job waiting at a company called Quantex a startup company in plant research; mostly for the tobacco companies.

"My Quantex...!" Michael responds with laughter. Derrick nods his head and looks at Michael for any sign of recognition.

Derrick turns to Michael "...don't worry 'we' turned the jobs down". Now Michael is truly hooked as he listens to Derrick's story that Paul and he both had offers from Quantex and that he couldn't quite get his head around 'THE BUSINESS' of agriculture.

Michael asks about the girl that Derrick mentioned 'Sarah', Derrick just responded that she is looking for a job teaching in Northern California. They guessed that they had, had enough of the 'Hippie' scene in San Francisco it seemed the tourist were starting to infiltrate especially the Upper end of the city. How housing around the campus had been too expensive for them and the Upper side of the city is cheap and artsy which had drawn in Sarah. How to them they could sense that the whole psychedelic scene as beautiful as it is – it is going to destroy itself. It is too 'counter' culture; the hippies'; the 'BE IN'; how the psychedelics are just too open, in a close society. The three of them went up to Emerald not to start anything but just to be, for the summer before they had to start 'their normal' job scene.

In those days they found Emerald strains with all the unrest of loggers and cattle ranchers. The new arrivals found it difficult to fit in and even harder to get any help when they needed it. Derrick and Paul, again with Sarah's urging, started a commune; more out of let's care for each other rather than being anything. Paul has family money, he has grownup on the richer side of life, Derrick is a child of the working class grew up in a Chemical industrial area and Sarah is raised in middle class family, her Dad owned a gas station and did car repairs. They had met one summer in one of those summers 'lets educate your children' camp when they were in High School. They quickly became almost inseparable as kids even though they weren't quite living next door - they found care, support, and friendship in just being the best of friends.

There is trouble in finding enough space to get Sarah's commune started – the cattlemen up there didn't see any need to support them – no money in it and the loggers truly disliked them – because they interfered in logging the "tree huggers" they called us. Paul hit on the idea of just buying some acres from a family forest- after the '62 flood there were ranchers and logging families that were still hurting. Paul talks his father into the idea of a long-term investment since logging is falling off and land is cheap. The three of them all had something to offer to really get a commune going – they turned their backs on the 'normal' job scene.

More kids started coming into the area on their way to Canada because of the war. The Vietnam War really started the communes and the exodus of the Hippies to greener peaceful pastures- they became stop over places; with vets coming back from Nam. The vets brought their marijuana from Nam tall lanky plants – more suited to the jungle. Paul hit on how the different strains of marijuana produced different plants and differing effects… that there must be something about the weed that caused it to be so radically different in production, size and effect.

Then of course there was 'Woodstock' in '69, which caused even more kids to come, followed by college riots that spurred even more kids to head north - that is when they knew that they had to stay. They found that they had been there for five years and developed something that works and life is good. And more and more kids came pouring in hiding out from the war and that drove all the kids north seeking shelter. The 'War on Drugs' didn't help the kids. Their commune was becoming over run with transient and kids just fleeing and not having a direction… all the communes seem to be a safe haven back then. But it is too much for them …so they gave away the commune land and sold the rest and moved further into the mountains deep in the Redwoods further north. "It is peaceful and away from everything, we made sure that no-one knew where we were – it is like we just left - with all the others going to Oregon".

Derrick finds he enjoys Michael's company as he drifts through time. "… but of course we had to make some money and we had established a fairly good business in the weed that that we were growing. It isn't great stuff but the demand is high and Paul began to 'fool' around with plant selection and crossbreeding.

"What happen to Sarah, is she still with you guys?" Michael wanted a bigger picture than just people growing weed.

Derrick's face turned ashen as he looked at Michael and says, "something's just don't workout". Michael realized that he had stepped on something that hurt and turned back to his drink. "Now, I'll tell you about why I am so curious - about you coming up here" Derrick says, as Michel sees Derrick's face harden and his jaw line stress under his bite. "You see some sales guy came up to Emerald from Quantex…" Michael eyes widen under the thought of another connection but this one sounded as if it would be menacing and Michael looked away into his glass. "Emerald had become it's own peace and love community only the peace and love sometimes collide. Every year, during the early days the marijuana growers got together and would throw a party in about late August when the crop is ripe and harvesting started. Rock bands would come up and after the third year no invitations were necessary - they just began to show up - and how good their crops were doing would determine the size of the party. Nothing like 'Woodstock' size but there were a lot of people - and the local cops had learned to just leave us be. Even a few of the cowboys and loggers would show-up even if it were just for good time party".

"Sarah and I had become quite an item," Derrick continued as the bartender kept things flowing "… we didn't marry but everyone took it that we were. Sarah taught classes to the younger kids – Art – and such; Paul and I would tend to the crops playing hide and seek with the Feds agents. But the 'Festival' time was different, it is all 'Live and Let Live' for three days anyway. Our life had become routine in it's own way and a small town had started to grow a few miles down from our road - nothing that would seem to infringe on our lives; but we added to it's economy – and that helps us fit in."

"The logging companies started doing business at the festival. It is after all something to show to business types from the small businesses to the ones in the bigger cities. Paper, Lumber, Agro-grow, Chemical, Fertilizer companies they would all come - always asking about the hippies and looking for a show. So it became normal for them to come to the festivals and with some business type – you could always tell who they were - always - so it really didn't bother anyone - 'Live and Let Live'. Well, one festival this Quantex salesman shows up with a few of the guys from the big lumber company. The Three Rivers Company on the first day – everyone could tell who they were – and it didn't really matter. Anyway on the second day this salesman returned in an outfit that made him fit right in with the crowd but he couldn't quite hold his own when it came to smoking weed."

Derrick continues "One day in particular he came over to the booth that Sarah had set up with teas and brownies of all type and strengths. 'He asked '... How much for the tea, my throat's sore from the coughing. Sarah sold him some 'special tea and brownies' thinking that he knew what she was giving him. But this guy, Ed, didn't know."

"…you say his name is Ed?" Michael asked;

"Yeah, is he still working at Quantex?" Derrick says worried that there is more than just a passing connection.

"I don't know, Quantex sales department is huge - with connections all over the globe". Michael quickly responds and tries to keep his question matter of fact. "What's his last name I can look him up on the company directory, if you'd like?"

"I'm not sure I just always remember his name is like some bird name 'something', you know, like the kind you use for hunting." Derrick studied Michael's face as Michael looked down at his drink

"…Sounds strange I'll look it up for you?" Michael says looking back at Derrick. Michael's field skills were ever sharp - but Derrick's were better – Derrick could see there is some connection but he couldn't tell just how deep it was.

"Well anyway …This Quantex guy stole Sarah away", Derrick decided to press Michael to see if he had cornered him.

"I'll see if I can find out what happen to him, if you like" Michael adds hoping there really is nothing to all of this.

"Nah, she has her life and I have mine" Derrick returns but with a softer inflexion in his voice.

Ed had wounded Derrick back then, in way that would change everything. "This Ed guy is a young star for Quantex then and he had convinced Quantex to let him get involved in field investigation of what other companies were doing - along with part of his sales job. This Ed guy is there getting information on the new field of selected plant growth for industrialized agriculture – lumber - to see what the competition is up to and get some business buzz going".

"Sarah was taken with Ed's naivety when she sees him sitting against a giant redwood with picked flowers around him; sitting there and just tapping his hand on his knee to the beat of the 'Folk Rock' being played at the concert. He seemed to have wandered well away of the general festival crowds and booths – some small distance from the booths in the Redwoods. Sarah wanted to get away from the booths, crowds and to put some distance from it all - and maybe she had just a little too much homemade beer; we'd had a big argument (one of many) over nothing important but she says she could feel us growing more distant. Sarah walked with a joint in her hand casually as ever taking a drag every now and then."

"As she wandered closer toward Ed, I guess he sees that her yellow skirt is almost translucent with the sun at her back; the silhouette of her body is a vision – she had a shape… Well, anyway seems Sarah sat down near Ed to see if he is OK and they got to talk. You know; 'look like the brownies' have helped your state of mind;' kind of things – she had away of smiling that would light you up. But the smiles were meant purely as a smile – nothing special" Derrick continues "…as she told me later - she found herself studying his face, slightly sunburn from the summer sun. Here let me put some aloe on your skin before you get a bad burn. Sarah was statuesque - people always thought she was taller than she was; she was the model of the beautiful Hippies. She had done some fashion modeling and photo shoots to help with school and had always had trouble with her beauty getting in the way." Derrick seem to really getting into the story he was telling "Anyway, she told me of how the whole Ed thing happened; she had taken some aloe from her skirt pocket and knelt to put the Aloe on Ed's forehead; as she knelt down. Her long blond hair fell down along one side – guess she didn't give any thought that her breast could be seen poking out of her cotton top – when she is bending over Ed – it exposed her small breast. Ed told her that her breast seemed somehow pure and he found himself staring down her blouse as she leaned over to rub the aloe on Ed's face." "Ed must have been transfixed by the vision and she reached around him to put some aloe on Ed's left cheek and ear, and he could feel her nipples against his skin. She says that Ed was over come with the vision – probably more likely the weed and Ed passionately embraced Sarah kissing her. But I guess to Ed's delight she didn't pull away as he had somehow expected but leaned into his embrace, her mouth opening as they kissed. Anyway they made love and it was quite passionate. I had gotten worried about Sarah – she isn't at her booth and I started looking for her – I guess they heard some others and me. Ed probably heard our feet stomping around - and heard her say loudly "shit" as she pulled herself off Ed. We could see Ed is pulling his pants up stumbling in the dry dirt. Ed had no idea what to expect- Ed knew if she were a Logger's woman he should be running as fast as he could. Sarah got up quickly picked up her blouse and pulled it on, running and crying up toward a hill and deeper into the forest towards our house." Derrick paused

Derrick continues "I just took a long look at Ed – Ed is taller and would have a much longer reach in a fight; but then I thought - what would I be fighting him for… the guy is probably just the innocent one. I saw he looked like he is the guy (some salesman) that the Logging Company had brought with them the day before."

I jumped down from this large stump I could see them from and asked, '…

You came here with the Three River company men yesterday, right?' The last thing I wanted was a dispute with the logging company and I'm sure he didn't want to get into anything with us locals; it might wreck his chances with the River Logging company.

Ed dusted himself with this 'oh shit' look on his face and says, '...Look I don't want any trouble I'll just clear out". Derrick says "I was pissed and I guess I showed it – except I was too stoned – so much weed there so I asked him his name".

He says 'Ed...Ed Falcon' or something like that. I let my anger show and just said 'look Ed, just clear out, and get out of Emerald'...! I could feel my anger begin to build more ...and knew I didn't want a fight - I just wanted to hit someone. I stood there and found my fist beginning to clinch. He asked '...what is your name ...if you don't mind me asking...?'. I yelled at him "Derrick", I thought he might as well know who he is in a formal way – I don't know - guess it is the weed in me - now that we' d been introduced" I told him "...get the fuck out of here", Derrick say in an angry voice ... and pointed toward the direction of the booths. Ed seemed like he is pretty stoned too he shook his head like he is trying to get a grip on reality. I thought fuck the last thing I need is a stoned asshole stealing my girl – anyway - with his long walking stride he quickly went out toward the dusty old road; Ed must be a proud person – but he didn't seem to want a fight either. Also he didn't seem that he is not afraid of one, and he looked back toward me while he walked away. And that is how I lost Sarah – and everything changed then." Derrick's face is ashen as he slugged down a gulp of cognac – but it seemed like he want to get it out of his system.

Derrick continues, "Ed seemed to have every intention of putting as much distance between himself and me as he could and as he walked up the dusty dirt path and he passed the booths where Sarah had worked."

"Ed glanced back as he passed the booth and suddenly walked into Tom," this tall heavy set guy with a long black beard, a man that appeared to be very much part of the local community. Tom seemed intent on blocking his way, and when I saw them I guess I yelled, 'Let him go...he didn't do anything".

"Tom says something like you're lucky Derrick spoke for you, as Ed climbed into his Cadillac rental, dirt and dust spread from his tires as he left." Sarah told me later Derrick continued "that Ed had finished up his business with the Three Rivers Lumber Company, I guess, and there is nothing left except to get to back to his business life – after his taste of the real life…"

"Ed just took off down the road when he must have seen this girl walking down the far steep and grassy hillside toward the highway - Sarah. Ed sees that it is Sarah and slammed on his brakes putting down rubber on the highway and spreading the gravel from his path on the highway shoulder. I had heard that she lived with Ed for a couple of years, had a kid – some real wow kind of place - and I see her photos in some fashion magazines. 'The Next IT Girl' the article says, with all the by-gone psychedelic nonsense decorations." Derrick says sounding like he needed a break from the past.

"So did you ever see her again?" Michael pressed and Derrick continued. "Sarah came back to Emerald some ten years later and opened a tourist style rock and jewelry store; but and I guess I was slow to make amends. Shortly, after Sarah left that summer, right during peak of the harvest; the biggest raid ever hit Emerald. The Feds used helicopters in this paramilitary style attack on grower's homes destroying pretty much everything. Not much of that town remains now but a few small shops. Some people were badly injured and there were two deaths and several homes destroyed. I knew it had to have been Ed's information because the loggers were part of the volunteers for the Feds. I just refused to believe the rumors that Sarah had anything to do with it or even that Ed would be that malicious; he told everyone, the information just got in to the wrong hands. There is an upside to the destruction; the ACLU stepped in and made demands for an investigation and even created the Medical Marijuana defense during the trial. There is a lot of press good and bad on both side but the best thing is that growers finally put their petty differences behind them and they all came together".

Derrick took a gulp of his drink and continued "The raid had given the Feds the type of major score they had hoped for; however, the repercussion carried far into the future. The Feds had laid waste to the Emerald pot growing industry and culture that is set to replace the dying Lumber Industry, that gave Emerald such fame, … and …destruction. There is not much left of the grower's little town every building, store, shop suffered losses or total destruction and the community knew it would never be the same. Most left and moved on to Oregon or onward to Canada; however, a handful stayed and Emerald's major underground economy is born."

"After the raid those that stayed" Derrick continued "… had to band together in order to stay and survive."

The memory of their meeting faded in to the highway, as the mile drifted along. Michael marvels at resiliency and creativity of Derrick's generation- and wondered what would be said of his generation – although the technology of his generation is no small feat. Different time different place – he thought with a smile. Michael had enjoyed his conversation with Derrick and felt sure that he would be able to find him.

As Michael started up the Kings grade he sees the new construction that would help ease the squeezing population growth. The big trees were now being cut again to make way for growth of a hopeful kind.

As Michael enters Ukiah for gas – the feel of the place is different than he had expected; the new growth didn't seem welcomed. No real friendly 'hellos' like he had expected. Then he looked at his clothes – city clothes he thought – 'I'll have to take care of that ASAP' he thought. The further North he pushed, the scenery turned prettier – in places he wanted to stop and take in the splendor of it all – so rural – the grassy wind swept hillsides – dark green forest – and even a redwood tree or two. But there is something about the people – the shops were touristy – and people hardly spoke to him. 'The suit I guess' he thought to himself - again. The strangest thing is the number of oversized 4x4 trucks and pickups, all covered in mud – but they were all new – even a number of small rental moving trucks. Then he thought of discussions with Derrick and smiled – 'getting into the pot world' he thought to himself. 'Derrick is right, the more North, he traveled the more beautiful the countryside became –more Redwoods – the people looked very rural the further he drove – but a casual rural with nice clothes – although not always clean.'

As he enters Barber there seems an even more unwelcome feeling that he sensed in the air; nothing he could grab or point to - but something just the same. He thought of his clothes again and why he had decided not to stop and get a change of clothes on route. But then he thought spending his money locally would get his answers quicker, than not. He could see that his concern of driving a new car would be lost on most everyone; the old cars he had expected just weren't around. The town did not appear as Ed had told him in his stories of Barber; poor and working class farmers. Rather a tourist town full of curious small stores catering to the visitors. However, there were inconsistencies that Michael could see as he slowly drove through town. Michael had expected that much of the town would be closed down for the winter; like some of the smaller towns that he had driven through, Willits and Leggett. This town seemed alive with people, although Ed's stories had been right about the town having only had one main street through town. But the town had a coffee shop, large grocery store, couple of banks and very clean streets; with well-marked storefronts.

He slowly feels more at ease as he drives further into Barber and sees the stores – even the makings of a small open mall; but still there is the curious puzzle of an added sense that something isn't quite right. Maybe just the climate – new place – old stores – he thought to himself – he is sure glad that the weather has been nice. Then he looks again at his rumbled suit and thought that at least he should take off the jacket; he didn't want to appear to be a flatlander but a tourist would do. The parking lot leading into the grocery store is large – few cars but large – probably large for the tourist, he thought. As he enters the store – it seemed like any other small town grocery store (just large) – music playing even current songs; and the people seem friendly enough; the store is fully stocked but with few customers. Well after all it is almost winter. He buys a few odds an ends – and thought he'd come back when he found a motel to stay at; but first it is taking care of his clothes – not that he is a clothes horse like Ed – but he did want to fit in.

PURPLE

The people in the grocery store suggest the Gun and Western store just a couple of blocks down if he needs any clothing. The afternoon air seems chilling for any walk so he drove the few blocks over the Gun and Western store. As Michael now got a closer look at the town he notices there were sidewalks of concrete and then of wood, old buildings mix in with new looking ones; it seems to be an odd mix without really much reason or maybe just in transition. He parks in front of the Gun and Western store and for the first time sees people smiling back at him. When he enters the Gun store he noticed that the storeowners were friendly but surprised to see any tourist this time of year. The people at the grocery store had been right – clothes of all types as long as you wanted western-wear. There is a comfortable feel to the store - he picked out what he thought would help him to blend in; jeans, red paid shirt and a hat like he sees a few folks wearing in town and as the owner suggest a new pair of lug boots. He noticed some hunting maps of the area at the store and picked out a few, that he thinks he might need. He didn't get much help though when he inquired about where Derrick lived – they were friendly but didn't seem ready to help him find Derrick. He decided to ask around town - after all he is a 'friend' of Derrick. After getting several versions of how to get to Derrick's place from the gas station and post office, he maps out a route that he thought might work out. His best find of the afternoon is Derrick's home phone number from the people at the real-estate office: he wrote the number on the back of the receipt. He calls but there isn't an answer so he left a message. Everyone had told him that his new rental car is not the type of vehicle he would be wanting for the roads in the backcountry especially if it rained. It is just noon and Michael (he had introduced himself as in town) thought he should try driving out today because rain is expected for tomorrow (beside he has Derrick's home phone number in case he needed help).

Derrick's place didn't really seem to him to be that far out of town- at least so it seems on the map, a drive out toward the ocean and a few side roads. As Michael heads out, he couldn't see any sign of storm clouds or rain, the road however showed that he missed judged the area. The road is rough and steep with tight hairpin curves that drove him deep into the forest of Fir and Hardwood trees.

By the time Michael got to Thorn Junction some forty miles from town and in the redwoods, Michael found that he'd been driving for just over two hours; but Michael thought his sightseeing spirit might have caused much of that time. As Michael heads past Thorn Junction he could feel the cold grayness of the storm clouds moving in and the road steepened with hairpin turns that would challenge the best of any off road vehicle; except that he is on the normal road, a road that everyone that lived out this way took day by day. Michael thought - clearly the people living out this far have a much different concept of 'going into town'.

Michael tries Derrick's phone a few times but finds that there is no cell phone signal; and feeling that he is better than half way, he pressed on. By the time Michael reaches the King's Peak Road for his turn off, the 'main road' Michael thought that he should of paid more attention to the townspeople advice. The grayness of the clouds had turned into the darkness of a coming storm that feels nearer to him as he climbs the mountain road. Michael had been told the King's Peak road is a main road that paralleled the mountain and hills to the ocean and that he would marvel at the views. However the only thing that Michael marveled at is a quick building foreboding storm and the sudden drop in temperatures; coupled with the fact that he didn't bring winter clothes suited for the area. Michael found it hard to believe the change in climates of the area; he had left a pleasant day for this – a storm that would descend on to the town to the East.

Michael finds now what people meant by 'his car isn't suited for the drive in this area'. The road would twist and turn in so many directions that he found himself guessing at the direction that he is traveling. His foreboding begins to build when he discovers that his GPS navigation system did not include this area; even though the rental car agent had assured him it would. 'City people' he thought and chuckles nervously to himself. Michael is however given some peace of mind when vehicles that he had to yield to on the road because of the speed, pass him by.

As darkness filled the sky and moves in to take over the day, Michael turns on his headlights and enters a split in the road that is not on his hunting maps. He thought that this is where he should turn back and head for shelter. Michael decides to stay on the better-surfaced road that hugs the mountain to the ocean. However, the paved road quickly gave out to a dirt road with deep ruts that reminded him of the ROAD TO HANA. He had been told not to drive on 'your rental agreement will not cover any driving that is done on this road' is the only reminder he felt creeping into his mind. With that storm seeming to build at every glance, Michael took to the West he finally thought that his adventure is no longer an adventure but perhaps a foreboding trip into the depths of Mother Nature. He found himself saying - 'if I can only get out of this I'll deposit large amount of money into the 'Save the Redwood' or whatever charity protects lost souls in this type of folly?'

Suddenly the road ended at a steep decline or at least a decline heading towards the West that Michael is not inclined to take. Michael pulled his vehicle to a stop and steps out to try and get his bearing – he is hit by a blast of cold air that seemed somehow fitting for his adventure. However, just over a rise to the northeast he could see what appeared to be headlights moving parallel to where he had come from; and he thought 'the road less traveled'.

Michael gets back into his car and slowly backs his vehicle up the steep dirt road. Michael's left rear tire begin to slip 'do I turn it to the right or to the left' he thought. In his moment of indecision he turned his wheel to the right and the wheel slipped off the dirt road; spinning in the darkness of the cliff face and brush below.

Suddenly, Michael noticed that headlights were headed down the road towards him; 'helpful friend or crazed grower' Michael thought to himself. The headlights of the vehicle flooded the inside of his car; making any thought of seeing anything impossible.

He heard two men yelling "put the emergency brake on…" They yelled and kept saying "put the emergency brake on'….". Michael barely knew where the emergency brake was – but he put the car into PARK. Then just as suddenly, he heard a noise in the back of the car underneath and felt the slight pull backwards. There is the tapping noise on the passenger window. Michael looked over and took a deep breath.

A very heavy-set man is tapping on the window and yelling "you got-a get out of the car now!" the man says sternly. Michael looked back and all he could see were the truck headlights in his rear window; he unbuckled the seat belt and slides over toward the passenger seat. The passenger door opens and the large man extended his large hand waving it as if he wants to help Michael out. As Michael slid into the passenger seat the man grabbed Michael's jacket and pulled him quickly out of the car.

Michael is pulled with such force he hit the dirt road so violently that his shoulder fractured and his head hit a rock on the far side of the dirt road. The man glanced a look at Michael and then continues to help get the car out the rut. The car rocked and strained. The front left tire slid on to a edge of the road with the left rear just barely on the dirt.

The large man raised his hand to the truck and gave a whistle and yelled, "Just let it go" and he bent down to see the J-hook straining against the weight of the vehicle and sees the cable is caught against the cars suspension.

"Kyle, get out-a way before it snaps". Kyle, being as large as he is could move when he needed to. "Lookout I'm going to let the cable go" the driver of the truck yells to Kyle; Kyle hit the ground and his face is covered in dirt. When the cable unwound from the gear spool the car went straight down crashing and rolling as it hit the hillside.

Kyle got up and dusted himself off, not that anyone would notice the difference. Kyle walked over to where Michael is laying and sees the blood on the ground dark crimson looking as the headlights reflected it back; almost a blackish tar color, except the road didn't have any tar on it. Kyle turned pale and weak at the knees. He bent over Michael and sees that he is still breathing; and breathe a loud sigh of relief.

The other man much more slender walked over to Kyle and says "…SHIT Kyle, he's dead"; Kyle just shook his head no. They see how Michael's shoulder is bent over

"…Kyle, we're just supposed to scare him and maybe rough him up a bit, just look at him" the slender man says (Frank). Kyle picked Michael up and carried him over to the pick-up truck bed; the wind from the ocean is hollowing in the darkness. "…He's go'n die for sure if we leave him in the bed" Frank says in a panic

Kyle gave him a grimmest smile "…then he should of gotten out of the car when I said - <u>GET OUT</u>" Kyle yells back at him. Kyle is not much for caring about how people felt about anything and this was to be 'dirty deeds done cheap" for Ron as far as he knew. Ron had given him a call about a Quantex guy out making inquiries about Derrick.

Kyle is Sarah's son and had never forgiven her for taking him from LA to live in Emerald; and never forgave his father, Ed, for the way he treated his Mom. Sarah knew that one day Kyle would step in front of Ed, when Kyle got angry at her; and that he is growing up BIG and fast. Yeah, Kyle grew up angry at the world; and large enough that most would step out of the way and just let him be. Ed had never married Sarah and didn't much care for Kyle even though it is his own son – he'd say '… the boy just came along at the wrong time.'

Sarah didn't want for anything while she was with Ed; except perhaps love and affection - but then she also made her own way as had Ed. Sarah found modeling or it found her through Ed's contacts and her beauty; and Ed climbed the corporate ladder because everyone loved Sarah. Sarah is genuine and attracted the struggling people and the beautiful people always paid her back – she would say 'got to do what's right because it will always come back to you'. Ed had benefited from Sarah's beauty and her wise ways. Like eye candy on his arm. It drew in the exec that would mean something at Quantex; yes she had beauty and brains. Quantex always gave Ed more latitude than anyone – the fair-haired boy and the golden-girl. Sarah enjoyed the modeling life style but could see first hand the effects it is having on Kyle.

"Let's get this guy over to Ron to see what he wants to do with him," Kyle said angrily.

"I think he needs a doctor or maybe a hospital" Frank said nervously and continued with a sigh as Kyle pointed for him to get in the car.

CHAPTER 6

DIRTY DEEDS DONE CHEAP

Kyle didn't much care about whether Michael lived or died, no one is going to do anything anyway 'it is not our fault', Kyle would say. They backed the truck on to the dirt road heading on down to Pleasanton where Kyle and the pickup bumps and pushes it way down the road into town. Kyle pulls into the house that he had bought when Sarah gave him money just trying to keep Kyle close to her. Kyle had done quite a job with the house – replaced the old siding with redwood and a redwood shake roof that held up well when the rains came in. Pleasanton is deep in the redwood "rain" forest and you could always count on the rain; 300 inches a year and it all fell as rain or snow during the six months where fall and Winter turned to Spring.

Kyle slammed the pickup door shut and starts off toward the front door of the cabin when Frank yells "Hey what about this guy in the truck?";

Kyle didn't bother to turn-around he just yelled back "He's probably dead by now all that bumping …" and he walked through the doorway.

Frank turns pale as he thought and jumped into the back of the truck bed. Frank leans over and turns back the paint tarp that Kyle had thrown over Michael's body and tied down. Michael's face is a purplish pale and Frank could see the blood is still wet. Frank reaches down and placed his fingers against the side of Michael's throat hoping that he could feel a pulse; but Michael is cold to the touch and his throat skin stiff – there is no pulse and Frank is weak at the knees.

Frank could hear the cabin front door slam as Kyle came back out side "…dead, huh…" is all that Kyle says.

Kyle has the cell phone in his hand and Frank knew it is only to be used for emergencies; although Kyle had never been real clear on what emergencies – he just knew that Kyle had asked him not to make any calls on it unless he is in serious trouble – then to press 6 and someone would always answer. Frank had always thought it is for an attorney or someone, so he never paid any attention to the phone – Kyle just had things that he did not want to explain and there is no use asking.

Kyle grips his cell phone tight and yells into it " We'll be at the gate in about an hour," Kyle yells strongly into the phone. "…Got to talk…. no this won't wait…"

Kyle continued toward the truck and opened the truck door. A damp mist filled the air with a musty smell of the old wet ground covered from a thousand years. The silence's of the night is broken by Kyle "Well you com' n or staying… we got to go…" Kyle yelled at Frank. Frank jumped into the passenger seat of the truck and sprang as he jumped off "…you covered him…right?"

Frank hasn't really but then he didn't want to go back into the truck bed where Michael's body laid; so he just looked at

Kyle and says "…he's dead…you…" – "I didn't do shit …his head hit the rock…I didn't…" Kyle responds angrily.

Kyle grinds the gears into reverse as Frank lunges forward, and tries to buckle the seat belt as the tires spun in the slick dirt. As they backed out – then slams the stick shift into first gear with a grin, Frank is forced into the back of his seat – while Kyle headed straight ahead into the night with the headlight beams caught in the dark mist.

Frank had gotten used to Kyle's temper but this is more and there is this dead guy they didn't know anything about except they were to told to rough him up and get him to go with them. This kind of work Kyle called "Dirty Deeds Done Cheap…" and Frank is just along for the thirty percent or so that

Kyle usually paid him – but he had not bargained for riding with a dead guy in Kyle's pickup.

"This isn't what I signed up for Kyle" Frank yells at him as the truck bounced along the backfire road.

Kyle slows the truck so that the truck didn't bounce as much and looks over at Frank with that stupid sneer that he would try to make – you knew he is pissed by the way he squints his eye with a sneer that would make you want to laugh but then you don't laugh at Kyle – especially when he's pissed.

Frank turned his focus back to the highlight beam into the darkness of the two-tire track dirt road; and says, "I'm just saying…".

"You'll get your 30% plus some. I just got to straighten this out…we were told to rough him up and to ask him about the Purple plants that Ron wanted to get into their business".

Kyle interrupts but in a softer tone. Frank knew he would be taken care of – which is fine – just as long as he could get away from the trouble when it starts; and he suspects there would be trouble.

Kyle, Frank, and the body head down the old mill road that would take them to the back area of Ron's place down across the King's road where Kyle only slows shortly to cross. Frank could feel the jars in his lower back and swore that he had wrenched his back pulling on the cable after they had let Michael's car go over the side.

"Quit your whining…." Kyle says angrily to Frank just over the roar of the engine as the car bounces on to Sparrow Creek Road that will take them to Ron's house.

Frank is glad when they finally get to the entrance road – a well-paved road-way that just appeared in the middle of some of the roughest roads in the forest. Ron had built a back entrance roadway so he could easily park the trucks needed to haul the marijuana out of his hidden warehouse.

Ron's property is an ambling area of backcountry where Ron has most of his private growing houses - those he reserves for his "special blend" as he calls it. The property is 405 acres of rough land all for Ron and it offers seclusion and just close enough to the highway where the trucks could get in an out. At the other end of his property lay Redwood Glenn and the Airstrip Ron had taken control of; there really isn't much that Ron didn't have his hand in – in one way or another. He got most of his product from pockets of small growers stretched throughout most of Emerald's backcountry; other people that had leased land from him and he in turned helped them with their product production for a nominal fee plus product – of course.

The Redwood Glenn area has always enjoyed the fruits of everyone's labors, including the tourist; with its four star hotel and lake where they held concerts and live theater outside. Ron has grown up watching Redwood Glenn thrive from all the money that seem to pour in from everywhere; tourist, loggers and growers all looking to spend money for the culture of the good life in the back country – and Redwood Glenn has it all. Ron had come to Redwood Glenn to make his own way in the only thing he knew, growing weed but in the process he exhibits his parents knack for making things happen. His parents had tried to give Ron the best that he would need … business education at Stanford but Ron couldn't be swayed from the backcountry underground industry of marijuana. With his skills he took over the old hotel and now a well known brothel that he operates …turned it into a four star hotel – Ron had always said that he stopped at four stars so not to draw to much attention to his life style. He even managed to get the local Indian tribe in Emerald to be recognized well enough to open a gambling enterprise in the hotel.

Kyle drove on to the black asphalt road that Ron had built in the middle of nowhere – up to the iron pole-crossing gate that marks the entrance. Kyle jumps down from the truck on to the solid black stretch of road and opens the phone box partially hidden behind a redwood tree – Ron had it put in during his spy period where 'everything is not as it seems' as he would say. Now most anyone dealing with Ron came through this way and the phone had seen a lot of use. Kyle was irritated with Ron and decides that this is something Ron is going to have to figure out; after all he had ordered them to harass Michael. Wanting to get some Purple marijuana plants and information or to scare them off. Until then, he could capture more of the Purple marijuana crop and cash in on the pharmaceutical business.

Kyle pulls out the receiver and presses the phone code – immediately a voice came on – "We have a package to discuss" and Kyle heard the electronic gate lock snap open.

Kyle pushes the gate open and then hears the surveillance gate slide open about a 100 feet down the road – Kyle had help with the security putting in cameras and lights around in the forest to monitor any activity.

Kyle gets back into his truck as two Rottweiler dogs walk towards the truck; Kyle knew as long as you stayed in the truck you were ok. The dogs followed the truck to the second gate where overhead lights shined down on his truck; he waves and smiles at the mounted outdoor camera.

Frank feels like the whole thing is the result of too much paranoia; and turns up the music "…I want your love.… I want your …" blasted over the truck speakers. The dogs stay behind the gate as it closed and Kyle drove down the road to a well-built wooden barn structure that had all the looks of being just that a barn. Kyle reaches behind the seat and grabs some pots with a PURPLE plant in them. He jumps out of the truck and slides the barn door open and Frank drives the truck in. Kyle sees two large lumberjack men standing in his way. Kyle nods his head to them as he walked in to the barn. The barn smelled of old animals and fresh hay and that unmistakable aroma of fresh cut Marijuana.

The two guards were there, Gregory & Stephen; Kyle says his hellos to them "good that you guys could find work" Kyle greets them – as he raises his large arms and the men pat him down.

"Nothing personal – Kyle" the one large man says to Kyle they knew Kyle is no man to be messed with but he knew everyone had a job even him.

Ron steps out from behind an empty cow stall that is used for storage. "I thought you were going to invite us up to the house, we brought you a special present", Kyle says as they greet each other with a handshake.

Ron had always said there is a lot you could learn from shaking another's man's hand. Ron had parted ways with his parents at an early age; home-schooled like most of the kids in Emerald. He was smart enough to get accepted at any university he applied to; except that he only applied to please his mother. Ron always figured school is a waste of time when there is money to be made; if he needs to learn something he would just figure it out. He had learned all he needed about growing weed from his experience and with his Mom's shrewd business sense; he made a formidable force in the business of the Emerald Marijuana industry. Yep there isn't anything it seems that Ron didn't have his hand in, some way or another; he had even started his own "growers collective" as he called it.

The collective is full of children of growers mostly and they didn't always have the stick-to-it attitude that their parents had; but they did enjoy the fruit of their parents labor even if they bent the rules from time to time.

Kyle explains what happened in a mater of fact manner about the death of Michael - Ron just stares at him. "Come-on your freaking me out" Kyle says to Ron with a chuckle "Shit happens".

To which Ron motioned to Stephen as he punches Kyle in the back kidneys knocking Kyle to the ground "Come on it isn't my fault…He hit his head on some rock …it isn't me" Kyle says hoping to plead his case.

Ron stares over at Frank who is being pulled out of the truck by Gregory "Hey man …it's just like he says…the guy hit his head on some rock. Check it out", Frank responds in a rather fearful manner – for this is more than he had bargained for 30% or not.

Ron responds to Frank, "Hey aren't you Joe's son…that asshole still pulling logs off that BLM land".

"Yeah…I guess so haven't seen him in a while" Frank responds nervously. Ron studied them both –

"…And you want me, to fix something that you broke… again?" Ron says staring at Kyle.

Then Ron steps away with Gregory and whispers something just below what anyone could hear. He could hear the word 'PURPLE'. Gregory goes to the back of the pickup and hoist Michael's body on his large shoulder. Michael's body is stiff with 'rigor' had set in.

Ron says, "…Where's the hat…" Kyle looked over at Frank

"I guess I'm not thinking…" Frank responds nervously. Frank opens the truck door and retrieves the hat from under the seat and walk towards Ron

"…and you're still not …" Ron yells at Frank as he motions to Gregory. "…. We didn't touch anything" Frank responds and notices that Gregory's hands were gloved with surgical gloves

Gregory takes the hat and carries Michael's body toward what appears to be an old tack room. "I'll do what I can at this end, but after this… you don't know me … look at me… and I better not see you anywhere in town". There is finality in Ron's voice.

Frank looked over at Kyle, who gave him a roll of the eyes look; and now looks somewhat more relieved that Ron seemed to have tempered his tone. There is nothing worse than being on the wrong side of Ron and no one knew that better than Kyle.

Kyle looks over at Stephen but he didn't return the look and Kyle began to wander how long Ron is going to be with whatever is taking so long, as the night is beginning to wear thin. They could hear other voices from the tack room and some scurrying about with the side barn door being opened then slammed shut

Ron's voice yelling, "I don't care what it takes clean him up".

An hour passes when Gregory emerges from the side area where the Tack-room is with Michael's body slunk over his shoulder. Kyle notices that the dust from the road had been wiped clean from Michael's jean pants legs and wanders if that is what all the fuss is about. Kyle thought about all those TV Cop shows where they dusted for the smallest of fibers but this is Emerald.

A woman that Kyle had seen in town jumps in the back of Kyle's pickup as another man hands her a large vacuum cleaner. Kyle recalls that he had seen them at the apartment building where someone hung a woman from a overhead fan and that the woman is the same person that had done babysitting for the dead woman's child – and suddenly the air seemed colder and more tense as the woman looked over at Kyle and gives him a wink.

Gregory carries Michael's body and lays him gently in the back of the pick-up and tosses Michael's hat back to Frank. Frank instinctively catches the hat as it flies toward him – but Gregory's glance at him and tells him "not to put it on his head but rather it is for something else" Frank watches as Gregory straps Michael's body into the pickup bed and covers him with a painter's tarp; and then fastens down the tarp so that there is no doubt that everything would stay in place.

Kyle stood yawning as he leans against the trucks wheel-well but he is soon call to attention when Ron reappears from the back of the barn carrying a plant, that Kyle recognized from the midnight raid they had on Derrick's orchid nursery. "You guys done good bringing the PURPLE plant" Ron said impatiently and added "But you messed up good with this Quantex person. You say it was an accident just stick with that story and you both should be ok."

CHAPTER 7

RON BAER

The town of Barber is beginning to settle in for the winter rains. The harvest is being completed and the product sold and as normal, Ron was in the mix of things. Most of the larger growers were wrapping up business in Amsterdam following the Cannabis Cup Expo or vacationing following the Island Conferences. There has been a lot of buzz created at this years Expo by a rouge non-entry to the Event. The day before, a cup is awarded to the grower producing the highest THC (Tetrahydrocannabinol (THC)– the active chemical in marijuana); a bud is rumored to have broken the 40% THC level. The bud had been brought to one of the more prestigious labs (Quantex Pharmaceuticals) at the conference. Vendors included growers as well as corporations such as Quantex. The bud is never presented for judging - as the owner of the bud says that he had purchased it on the street from an unknown party. However, by presenting a bud to the Quantex Lab any remarkable findings were sure to be printed in the Weed Times. At the conference the bud owner had picked up his test results and simply left, which in itself created a great deal of speculation about the buds origins. When word of the buds qualities were presented to the Cannabis Cup Board, the bud is dismissed as it's origins could not be verified; however Weed Times gave the bud full press coverage. Speculation grew that the bud had been one of Derrick & Paul's creations or some other big producer to cause a stir at the Expo among the participants. Later Weed Times confirmed this after extensive testing - the Quantex Lab verified the bud's chemical properties and the buds botany fingerprint.

The bud had the immediate effect of dropping the over-all pricing of premium quality THC buds; as the larger buyers waited for an announcement by the grower of the bud's ownership. However, there was no announcement and that caused the bud market to be extremely frenetic with wild daily swings in the pricing of premium buds and the rumor mill is in high gear. It is speculated that millions were made and lost at the Expo depending on the daily and sometimes hourly rumors that circulated.

Derrick & Paul were not seen at the Expo but rumored to be in the Islands planning for the conference of the 'Organized Growers Coop'. But … there were "Recognized" members of Derrick & Paul's at the conference to assist in completing further transactions that were needed; however, they had no authority to negotiate or offer any 'product news'. This situation caused further speculation to rampage through the Expo and Ron's people were at the ready to report the news to Ron. As is the usual practice, once a transaction is completed and funds traded, there is no refund or considerations offered, unless the board arbitrator deemed it necessary; which took a full vote of the Expo Board. This even further exacerbated the Expo when private persons holding "contracts" found that on any given day they could double their money buy selling the contracts to other parties – although it is forbidden by the Expo Board; but had become a backroom underground practice.

The Growers Conference had been organized by Derrick & Paul since the early days of the 'Nixon War on Drugs'; when a small group of growers were arrested on Federal 'Rico' charges – and while the charges were dropped it had put a chill on any large gathering of growers. Paul however through connections in France found suitable "accommodations" and "amenities" on one of the French Polynesian Islands; and of course the conference is never in the same place from year to year. Derrick & Paul (D&P) stay out of touch from the general Expo crowd which left many of D&P people also out of touch. The whole situation so outraged the Expo Board that they threaten to sanction D&P; however this soon died away when Jessie Hinkle (a widely respected member of the D&P organization and an Expo Board member) suggested that they wait until the Island Conference.

The Island Conference is made up of small and large growers the largest grower in Emerald is Ron Baer. Ron is a product of Emerald; well educated at Stanford and came from family money. Ron's family had made quite a fortune from buying and selling lumber acreage and the Baer family was known for it's less than honest dealing with Redwood Lumber. The family owned the biggest Bank in the town as well as large tracks of acreage in Emerald and had established an Indian Casino just outside of the town of Barber. Ron Baer was the oldest of three sons and ran the Casino and is the largest distributer of local Marijuana in all of the area.

"You have to have more information on this new strain of Marijuana that they talk about in the Weed Times - PURPLE" Ron said to Jessie angrily and continued. "I don't care what it takes I want that plant."

"Derrick has the plant I told you that; Why don't just contact him?" Jessie said in a stern voice.

"Just get me the plants" Ron responded and continued "40% THC is unbelievable I have to get a piece of that action before it spreads too far. People are already talking about waiting to see what the price is. This could really put a dent in my business…".

"I'll do what I can maybe you could see what the fire claimed, your boys sure did a nice piece of work" Jessie responded trying to calm Ron down.

"Yeah but I haven't seen the plant that they were suppose to get for me and I don't think they would have time to make off with too many plants – I hear they were pretty busy" Ron responded. Ron remembered he had the one plant that Kyle had brought him but he needed more and wanted everyone to believe he did not have anything to do with the plant.

Rumors of all varieties abound at the Expo; there were even threats on Jessie and his group. Anonymous threats were even made against Derrick & Paul. Some had lost millions and were not about to standby and let Derrick or Paul attempt to corner the market as some thought.

Most of the threats were not taken seriously until Corbin, one of Ron Baer's closest "friends" and trouble maker, made a suggestion to Jessie that "they" all hoped Derrick or Paul had nothing to do with the premium pricing swings that were taking place. Corbin had always been one of the 'dirty deeds done cheap' sort - this added to the darker side of the growers mystery; and many attributed some of the deceased persons to his handy work – he is the subject of many Emerald investigations. The rumors were not easily quieted, and the Expo was in complete turmoil until Quantex had agreed to fully test the bud and make their findings available to Weed Times and any other publication that desired the information.

The incident at the Expo might of really gotten out of hand at the Island Conference had Paul not offered to make D&P financial books available, if other members of the organization would do likewise. There is a substantial grumbling, however no member is willing to make such an agreement; especially Ron Baer. Ron has been known to try to affect the premium pricing on more that one occasion and has been publically sanctioned once; although he never made public the full extent of his operation or its clients.

Following the Island conference, life among the organization and Emerald returned to a tentative normalcy of Emerald's underground economy. However the whole furor is stirred up further with the publication of the Quantex Lab results in the Weed Times. The lab reported that the PURPLE Marijuana buds had 40.7% THC levels; shattering the long sought after barrier that is once thought to be unachievable.. D&P as well as Baer continued to offer no information regarding accepting or denying the ownership of the bud; however their concerted actions did bring stability to the premium bud market. Further stability to the market is added when neither of them or any other large genetic dabbling growers seem to add to their wealth or make the 'books' unavailable. The whole community decided to hold their breath and took a wait and see attitude.

CHAPTER 8
THE LAST RAID

Lee had told Donnie about the War on Drug days in Emerald and how Lee had been "requested" (back in the day as the kids would say) to join in the "round up and eradication of the evil pot growers". Lee had been recruited to join because of his knowledge of the Emerald back roads. The Feds had stepped up their efforts to bust as many growers as possible.

One summer, the growers had set up their warning system using local radio stations to broadcast the Feds helicopter positions and movements. Lee had just started as a Deputy Sherriff in High Country married with two young boys he could ill afford to say no – no matter what his politics were.

One faithful day the Feds setup a strategic diversion using multiple helicopters with ex-Vets as pilots, and Veterans to man 4x4 pickups to get through the tough terrain; it is to be a follow-up to their Barber raid the year before which had drawn so much criticism for their tactics. The Feds had pulled out all the stops ex-military; with County and local Sherriff were involved in the raid. They knew the grower had moved from the Barber area over the past year and had moved to Pleasanton where they established a small community. The Feds knew Pleasanton would be more difficult due to the terrain and back-road escapes; but they figured one more large raid and the growers would be forced to move out.

The growers helicopter spotters did their best, when they recognized the diversionary tactic from their days as an US Army grunts in Nam they call it as they see it. The helicopters came down from Northern Emerald as they usually did but instead of heading due south they circled west toward Elk Point; that is the diversion. The spotters picked them out as they swung West low over the road that led to the ocean; there are small growers off to South but Derrick & Paul knew they would be heading for the prize and would swing back to the North. The small growers had decided to abandon their crop just in case; however Derrick is right; they swung back North down the only surface road into Pleasanton. After the Barber raid Derrick wanted escape routes but no escape routes that the Fed could come up with; for Pleasanton there is one main road in and out. The Pleasanton pike as people called it is hardly a road; it is part dirt in the summer and muddy ruts during the winter. In most places a steep dirt road would shake you to your bones if you were not prepared.

Lee tried to tell them that taking people on the road is folly and the only way in would be helicopters; but the Militia didn't listen. The Feds had a small group of FBI agents but had deputized a small army of locals; mostly cowboys from the ranches and out of work loggers. The FBI had a troop of personnel that wanted the Hippies off their turf and out of Emerald.

The Pleasanton pike follows the ridge line of the small group of mountains; but then it came down the mountain ridges to the flats where Pleasanton lays nestled on what used to be cow country – but it was sold off when the family wanted to retire and Paul came through with the cash they needed. The road took a steep pathway, descending off the mountain ridges and to a gentler slope grazing land; it is there that Derrick decides to meet. Derrick setup a single locked steel road bar across the road.

As the Feds bounced around in their jeep 4x4, they see the steep decline into Pleasanton and could feel in more ways than not this is going to be difficult and that Lee is correct. The problem with being correct after the fact is that you are stuck; the Feds had to continue down to the flat grazing pasture in order to turn around - there is no backing up. The senior agent called for Lee to take the lead jeep in case there are problems. Lee is reluctant but followed orders.

They slow as they approached the road bar; Lee knew it is new and there is going to be trouble. "This is your war" he yells back to the senior agent "you'll have to open the gate I have no authority" Lee continues.

As the senior agent exits his jeep Derrick & Paul step from behind the gate unarmed; "This is private property; we'll let you turn back and we'll all call it a day," Derrick yelled at the agent.

The agent continues toward the gate and in a deep authoritarian voice and says, "I have a search warrant to travel these roads to search out any illegal drugs or plants you might have on the property."

The agent ordered bolt cutters to cut the lock off the gate. Derrick responded "I have the right to defend my property" and with that two very large armed ex-marines step in beside Derrick and Paul. The helicopters tried to swoop down but there isn't any clearance. The agent gave the order to drive through the gate – when four additional ex-marines in old army fatigues with a marijuana plant leaf on their shoulder came out of the woods to stand behind Derrick & Paul.

"Is that you - Doug you dickhead" came from the driver of Lees jeep? The ex-marine standing next to Derrick chuckled.

"What ya doing siding with these fools…fool" the driver stood up in the jeep yelling.

"Sir on the ridge", crackled over the army walkie-talkie radio in the jeep, "there are two snipers to your right; and another on the far left ridge, with what looks to be a Browning .50 caliber heavy gun mounted with a sight. Over" the radio crackled as the helicopter flew low over the ridge, and everyone turned in the direction of the helicopter.

"Senior …Agent" yelled Paul in response to the helicopter;

"…the Gunny on the left ridge has…" Derrick cut Paul off in mid-sentence "has instructions to do nothing except defend himself" Derrick quickly responds.

"Look, no one wants any trouble; we just want to live in peace and grow our weed to make a living…",

"…Is that all this is about are some marijuana plants…?" Someone yelling from the second jeep cut off Derrick.

"You says …this is…oh this stinks …I didn't sign up to get shot at over some damn plants". Their chuckles and acknowledgement from men on both sides.

"…Hell …Michael… we fought together…in Nam", "…and I saved your sorry ass…" came another response. Soon it became obvious to everyone except the Feds that this "raid" is over.

"Listen up we got grub …some weed and a few chicks that are tired of looking at our sorry…asses" Derrick yelled over in Lee's direction. Several of the Deputized cowboys jumped down from their jeeps and started walking towards the gate. A large logger turned to stand in the way…the senior agent said "Stand down". The loggers were invited as well as the Federal agent but they decided that they would head back. The loggers still bore ill feeling toward the Hippies for stealing their work "Tree huggers…" came a yell as the jeeps turned around in the grassy meadow.

Lee and Derrick never really became friends but it is obvious that there is an understanding; and that some agreement (Live and Let Live) had been made. No one quite knew what the agreement was but times got easier for both sides; including the cowboys and loggers.

CHAPTER 9

GONGORA

Donnie settles into to his more normal routine he'd been accustom to over the last couple of years; traffic accidents in the winter rains, road closures for mud, rockslides and the occasional traffic stop for speeding. Most of the time Donnie paid little attention to the traffic during the winter. He knew most everyone - and could simply give them a warning – or call in or mail the citation to them – it just seemed to make everyone's lives simpler. The days of highway harassment and speed traps were long since over; as well as the spot checks of rental trucks for Marijuana plant swords in four-foot tall closet hanger boxes.

Donnie sits parked on the northbound side of the small hill that slops away from the Barber exit. Most locals knew if he is out, that it is a good place to find Donnie. They would honk their horns or flash their lights as they pass by. During the summer Donnie would catch tourist-leaving Barber anxious to get to the Redwood Park - Avenue of the Giants; just a few miles on up the highway. Donnie would stop the tourist and asked if they had stopped in Barber and if they had, he'd give them a warning most times. In the winter it is about the only place to catch speeders that had not been to Barber. Donnie had his educational tapes playing in the cruiser and would play them repeatedly to make sure he hadn't missed anything.

As Donnie is about to pull out, head down and go back to town "231B up, over" came the scratchy squawk over Donnie's radio. It meant a likely speeder is heading his way; the Mendocino Deputy had not stopped him. Donnie turned off the educational tape and watches the road; sure enough there he is a black four-seated Limousine in his side mirror. Donnie checked the speed radar and it showed 90mph; "Damn" Donnie says under his breath "I'll have to get out and it will just be some State guy or someone important going up North". But no signal came over; Donnie switched on the over-head flashers to pursue and started calling it in when the limo pulled over. Donnie called in the plate and TTC number and then punched in the information – Limo service out of San Francisco. Frustrated Donnie got out of the cruiser he didn't even bother to pull out his violation pad; he thought 'it'll just get wet in this drizzle'.

Donnie approaches the vehicle and sees the driver's window slide down. 'Well at least he has some manners' Donnie thought. Donnie could see the drivers face in the limo's side mirror; the driver is dressed in a black limo style uniform with his cap still on 'must be someone real important'.

"Sorry officer" the limo driver says; "...I'm carrying Mr. Ed Falconer from Quantex Corporation.... " Donnie looks and listened as the driver explains "...that Mr. Falconer has lost contact with one of his employees that was headed up this way ...".

The backside window rolled down as a white thin faced man smiled at him "Hello, Officer I'm Ed Falconer, I'm trying to find some information about an employee of mine...Michael Swartz". Again Donnie looked and listened as the thin-faced man explained that they were looking for the Southern Emerald Sherriff Station.

Donnie listens and realizes that they are looking for Barber and just didn't realize it. As the thin faced man smiled, Donnie says, "The sub-station is in Barber, you just missed it." He waited for the acknowledgement to make sure they were who they say they are. The thin-faced man says "Officer, may we follow you back to Barber, perhaps you can help us", the man's face had a sense of urgency and relief on it. Donnie nodded his head and suggested that they follow him.

Donnie hasn't forgotten about the John Doe they found at the Park entrance. He couldn't shake the idea of a vision of him sitting on the top of the marker step. He has followed up with Joe about the body; but Joe didn't have much to offer except that he is sorry that he lied about not touching the body. When Joe sees that the body had fallen, he says he just "…wanted to get a closer look…" and he "…did not touch noth'n…" Donnie played the tapes inside his head and just winced a smile. The Feds had not come up with anything "…we are working on it, Sheriff Blevins…" is all Donnie ever got.

Donnie believes Lee hasn't told the Feds about the flower but the Sheriff did say there is an odd perfume smell to his shirt pocket but nowhere else on him; and the smell is most likely some kind of flower or perfume. They are right it is a particular smell; one that Lee had committed to memory.

✻ ✻ ✻ ✻ ✻

The rain starts to let up as Lee left the last of the Redwoods and approaches Fortuna. Fortuna had always been considered the beginning of Northern Emerald and that sat just fine with people of Fortuna. Fortuna had been a mill town; however, after the mills closed the ranchers had taken the town back and the pick-ups took over.

Lee got off the Fortuna exit and passed by the old closed down abandon mills and the hillside they left behind; still healing from the scars of clear cutting. The day is overcast, the kind that threatens of rain but it didn't; and the chilled air is full of moisture from the onshore breezes that brought in Southern Emerald's storms. Lee thinks it is a fitting day for investigating something to take his mind off the glum of the day.

Lee bumps along the narrow farm road that leads to town; meeting glances from farmers in their pick-up as they speed past him.

"Sarah's Flowers and Plants" the sign read as Lee pulled on to the gray gravel shop entrance. The store stood neighbored by a small drycleaners and a barbershop with a small grocer. It is a pretty normal mix of small stores for

Fortuna – nothing like the tourist shops of Barber (this is a community). Lee takes a deep breath as he exits his vehicle; the last time he had talked to Sarah he had asked her out - she says '...No nothing settled from her break-up..'. Lee shook his head and thought a call on her is overdue. They had been an item for a short spell but she wanted no part of Emerald. Lee steps on the wooden (red-wood) sidewalk and hears of the jiggle of the doorbell as he entered the shop. Sarah always has the best flowers in the Fortuna area – some would say in all of Emerald. The shop aroma fills the air a heavy mix of roses, the deepness of sage and the perfume of the orchids. Sarah has always had orchids – she only had a small growing area and the variety of orchids seem to be out paced for the small growing space she had. She loves her orchids even had an established 'orchid hospital' as she called it.

Sarah glances up at Lee as he walks into the shop; he had taken his time coming in the store – partly for his own composure but also he didn't want to appear that he had just dropped by.

He returned her smile; as she says politely "...let me just finish wrapping this...";

"...no problem, I got time..." Lee says in reply.

Lee strolls along the aisle his boots echoing on the wooden floor; glancing back at Sarah as he could. Sarah wore her slacks a little tight and she had her usual V-neck sweater top on with the hood in the back - so she could comfortably go outside when she needed to. She has told Lee the V neck is for the customers; it helps the sales, Lee could see her point times were tough and it is winter – with no tourists.

Lee drifted toward the orchids; think if anyone would have a clue as to the origins of the flower Sarah would. Lee fumbles with the plastic evidence bag in his deep jacket pocket as he smiles at Sarah.

"Got something I'd like you to look at, if you have a moment." Lee says as Sarah approaches and he pulled the evidence bag from his jacket pocket.

"...And here I thought this is going to be a social call..." Sarah smiles and quip's back to Lee irritated at what she thought is Lee's attempt to make up a reason for seeing her. "…You know that … you can stop by anytime, you don't nee…" Sarah stopped as she sees Lee pull the evidence bag from his jacket. "…Oh really do ha…" she stopped and began to chuckle "…does anyone teach you guys how to store perishable evidence…"

Lee looked down at the bag "…maybe you should teach some classes…". Sarah half smiled as she took the baggie from Lee

"…I just wan…" Lee began.

"Don't worry officer I know how to handle perishable evidence…" Sarah says and lays the bag on the flower-cutting table and opens a lower drawer – taking a very long pair of forceps looking tweezers. She carefully opened the baggie and smiles. "…This will cost you…". Lee manages to grim a smile;

Sarah says "…I thought you didn't care for orchids…what is it you say; …Oh yeah 'they look too fake" Sarah chuckled and added "if you want you can leave it with me and I'll get it all IDENTIFIED…" Lee gave her a glancing look "…well that is what you want …RIGHT?" Sarah finishes smugly.

"It's evidence for a murder case"…. Lee says. The Sheriff Blevins had given Lee the task of finding all he could, as he did not have the resources to process any evidence quickly. That Lee could get the information on that what is needed quicker; Lee thinking he really needed her help; taking it over to Emerald State would draw attention. "I just need to know what it is and where it might of come from" Lee managed his best official voice considering the situation.

Sarah says, "This must be important and that probably no one else knows about this evidence…?" she smiles. Then she takes Lee's hand in hers and rubs his hand on her cheek. "I thought you were angry with me…stuck on being in Emerald and wanting you to come up here…" Lee is in love with Sarah – and she knew it - but the boys and the job came first and she knew that too.

Sarah hopped up on the Cutting Table and put Lee's hand on the top of her thigh. "Can I have the evidence back tomorrow AM…"

Sarah smiled and says, "…Aren't you going to stay over…" and took Lee's hand in hers.

Lee looked into her blue eyes and says, "Wish I could. Really …but I left Donnie alone in town and then…"

"And then there's the boys" Sarah finished Lee's objection; pulling Lee in closer between her legs and hold his hand against her cheek..

"Damn it …Sarah…" Lee blurted out with a glimpse of a smile; and finished with "…a rain check …OK?"

Sarah smiles and says, "…Sounds like the rain is here now, how about I close up the shop". Just then a woman came in with some orchids in her arms. Lee instantly pulls back, as Sarah jumps off the table.

"I hope, now is OK; with the rain being … Oh hello Lee" the lady responded as she looked over at Sarah. "Maybe tomorrow would be better…?"

"Hey Kiki" Lee responded knowing Kiki from Barber;

Sarah responded with "no let's do it now, maybe we can get Lee to give us a hand" Sarah responded. Kiki lays down the two orchids that she had in her arms – and gave Sarah a glancing look. "No problem, what do you need…" Lee knew by the type of cab over pickup truck that she is hauling plants from some-where; probably Derrick's hothouse.

Sarah takes Lee by the hand and urges him outside to Kiki's truck. Kiki went around to the back and opened up the hatch. Lee had almost expected to see marijuana plants the way both of them were acting; but there on the truck bed were orchids of all size containers and varieties.

Lee says, "Now I know you know …" Sarah quickly says "…and it's our secret… right…?" Lee nods his head in acknowledgement as Lee began to take the potted orchids from the truck bed; and suddenly he noticed that sweet perfumed smell – that had come from the John Doe's shirt. Lee reaches back to the small plant and says,

"I can take another…I'll be careful" as he gives Sarah a look.

Lee carefully took the plants inside and notices Kiki and Sarah joined in conversation. He quickly laid down the small plant and bent down to inhale the perfume aroma coming from the flowers.

"It's a 'Gongora' I have no idea where Derrick got it from" Kiki says to Lee sharply. Lee could hear the crackle of the radio from his 4x cruiser;

"I better get that …I left Donnie alone in town…" Lee says hurriedly running towards his cruiser.

"Yeah Donnie, over, what's up…over" Lee closes the door to the cruiser as he speaks with Donnie advising that he would call back on the cell phone. Lee yelled over to Sarah "…got to run …Donnie's got some big shot over there that wants to…."

"I know …I know…" Sarah says as she waving him away. Lee speeds off forgetting the evidence; but he quickly spun around and ran back into the shop. Sarah is just opening the evidence bag a little – and Lee quickly grabs the bag from Sarah – who has a surprised look in her eyes.

"Almost forgot, I'll call you" Lee says hurriedly thinking 'did Sarah smell anything'? As he put the flower in the baggie and in an envelope and carefully stuffs the evidence baggie into his jacket and pulls away. Lee put on his over-head flashing lights for his drive back to Barber; it is not so much his hurry to get back to Barber as it is haste to leave Sarah's shop. The thought of Sarah being involved made him very nervous; now he felt that he would be compelled to make a call on Derrick.

CHAPTER 10
ED & LEE

When Lee got to Barber he found that Donnie had taken off to lunch at Marge's Café. Lee is anxious to find out more about the orchid plant and turns on his desk computer. The Sherriff Substation is small and tucked away off the Main Street down a side street staying just close enough to be present without really being seen. The Office is small with a part-time dispatcher and two desks that sit off in the back, and Lee's Office or 'CUBE' as Lee referred to it. There is a jail that is used mostly during the summer Festivals; one large cell for disturbing the peace type and two smaller ones for the more serious cases. Lee poured through the Internet sites trying to find out all he could about the mysterious orchid. However, all he could find is that it is rare, extremely fragrant and from the jungles of some island off of South America.

Then something caught his eye when he sees that the plant is referred to as the 'Punch and Judy Orchid, by turning the flower on it's side you could see the two quarrelling figures appearing to be battling it out with each other – a very odd reference which gave Lee pause to smile thinking of the irony.

Donnie calls into Lee on his cell to see where Lee is and explains about the new visitors … but that is the last thing on Lee's mind … to entertain some business prospector from wherever. As Lee got up from his desk he could hear Donnie's voice outside talking about the town businesses – his voice is unusually loud. Lee only hoped that Donnie's discussions did not include any police or town business as he had done before. The town business people have asked that Donnie never again talk to visiting business people.

"Ok that about does it for me I think that the man you want to see is here" Donnie says as he opens the door and looked over at Lee with a smile that looked like the 'Cheshire Cat of Alice'. After all the pleasantries and exchange of business cards are done,

Ed faces Lee straight on and says, "Do you know a Michael Swartz"? Lee had forgotten how straight forward and 'cut to the chase' business executives were … refreshing but also disarming – it is a straight YES or No question and there is nowhere to dance to. Lee studied Ed's face which appeared hard with age and the battles of business.

"No, should I, the name does not ring any bells" Lee immediately responded adding "…is there something I can help you with?".

Ed sat down in the chair in front of Lee's desk and peered toward the computer, "I was here years ago once during a festival of sorts and a man named Derrick helped me out of a jam" but then went on to explain that one of his field AVP had gone missing, perhaps in this area. Ed placed his brief case on the chair next to him and pulled out a photo of Michael and handed it to Lee. Lee is taken back by the frankness of Ed's take-charge demeanor and decides to keep his distance for it seems that Ed had an agenda.

Lee surmises that Michael might be his John Doe; just then Donnie came back in from the back door – still wearing that Cheshire cat smile. Lee glanced over at Donnie and motioned him over to his desk. Lee showed Donnie the photo and Donnie's face turned cold – an expression that Lee had never really seen.

It looks like we found our John Doe" Donnie says with a stone face – but Lee could see that Donnie already suspected this is going to happen.

"I'll get the information and call up to Eureka" Lee says. "That's fine" and gave Donnie a raised eyebrow look of 'done ok - but - we have to talk'. Donnie escorted Ed to his desk and signed on to his computer and went back to wearing that smile.

Lee is feeling more comfortable about Donnie and his abilities than he had been and studies Donnie while he types Ed's information into the computer. Lee thought maybe this is the turning point for Donnie. A sudden relief came over Lee while he realized that they were becoming a team; Donnie is going to make it as he mumbled "…now what do I do" to himself and took the cell phone off his desk and walked slowly to the back supply room. Donnie glanced over as Lee left his office and headed to the back – and feels this is how it's all done as he dropped the Cheshire smile and realizes with his stone face that this is serious – but as Lee had told him 'don't jump unless you know for sure what you're jumping into'.

Lee isn't gone for a minute when he came back and says to Donnie in a matter of fact way "I got to get back up to Fortuna and you can finish up here … you need anything more?". Lee studies Donnie and realizes things are going to be OK.

"Nah you go on I got this" Donnie returns and Lee winces as he thought that is a little too informal but that is just the rough edges of something he would work on with Donnie. Donnie caught himself and gave a smile to Lee as Lee headed toward the door.

Lee had called Sarah to see if she is still there at her shop; the phone rang a while and went to message – Lee looks at his watch; just three and thought she should still be there – maybe just busy and hung up without leaving a message. Sarah will know he called by the caller ID; the thoughts of Sarah flooded Lee's head as he started his cruiser and headed out of Barber.

Ed sits … a little taken back that Lee has left and feels maybe he had underestimated the sheriff – if so it would be the last time as he says hurriedly to Donnie. "…Will all this take much longer? I'm anxious to know if your John Doe is my employee". Donnie slowed his typing speed and says just a few more questions Mr. Falconer. Donnie knew that he needs to give Lee sometime otherwise his Mr. Falconer would catch up to Lee going same way.

Lee put his foot on the accelerator of the cruiser and heard the engine roar as he headed on to the Highway with lights going; wet gravel slipping under the speed of the cruiser's tires. Lee grips the steering wheel and watches as his speed increases thinking if Sarah is involved maybe she didn't know she is involved. He'd be damn angry if she knew and is just being tight lipped. He bit down on his inside cheek as he accelerated speeding past the Park's Granite Marker. He looked back to see if Ed's black limo is anywhere back there. He picked up his radio mic and calmly says 10-36, over.

The gravel squawk came over the office radio. Donnie casually got up and walked to the office radio at a center desk. Donnie acknowledge the 10-36 (confidential information) and replies 10-98 15 (meaning assignment would be completed in 15 minutes);

Lee responds "roger that" and accelerates into the steep left curve where they had seen the two black vehicles coming with the Eureka Sherriff. Lee thinks if he just had 5 minutes that is great but Donnie holding him there for 15 minutes would be all right – Lee is feeling better about Donnie. Lee looks back and could see only the spray from his cruiser and nods his head to himself.

Ed taps his fingers on the desk as Donnie slowly walks back; "we saw a motel as we pulled into town …would you recommend it?" thinking he would use the excuse that he has business to attend to. Donnie didn't miss a beat as he told Ed about the remodeling that had recently been done on the motel after the owners had come into some money. Ed sees the time slipping away and got up saying "I really must go; we'll be at the motel should you need anything further". Donnie never had a person just get up and walk out on him but it didn't seem as if he could stop Mr. Falconer.

"Ok, if there is anything more I need I will call you…" Donnie tried to think of something as Ed strode across the floor using the full extent of his 6' 6" frame as the chauffer opened the door for Mr. Falconer's exit; and Donnie could just make out "thank you officer" as the door closed.

Ed tells the limo driver to be ready by 8am tomorrow and to see if he could rent a 4x4 in town and to get some good maps of the area. Ed then checks into his room and grabs his cell phone from his briefcase – and pushes in some numbers. "Kyle, I have to know where this Derrick lives" Ed is almost yelling into the phone. Ed wrote some information on the pad of motel stationery lying on the desk. "Now are you sure" Ed says firmly, "well you better be!" and put down the phone.

✳ ✳ ✳ ✳ ✳

As the day comes to a close, Lee thinks back on when he first saw Sarah. Sarah drove from Fortuna down to Barber, and the moment Lee sees her he was smitten. Sarah looked every part the newcomer in her dress and attitude; but she also had an air of mystery like she fit right in. Lee found out that Sarah had left Los Angels to raise her boy in Northern Emerald, that the drugs and gangs had just been too much. They dated a few times but Lee's occupation and need to stay in Emerald overtime started to drive a wedge between them. Her son is in and out of trouble and Lee did manage to help from time to time with any Northern Emerald issues.

However, when her son left from high school things got real tough for Sarah and she asked for Lee's help; and he managed to get the boy a job cleaning up at one of the Mills. Over time Lee found out that Kyle joined another logging company working in the forest cutting trees. He is working with the group of loggers that got a little rowdy in town, that they were just trouble, a weed group that just spelled trouble for him.

✳ ✳ ✳ ✳ ✳

As Lee arrives at Sarah's flower shop in what he thought must be record time and bolted into her shop and upon seeing Sarah he yells, "You had bet….". No sooner had Lee started his question than Sarah came running straight at Lee and jumped into his arms - face to face him wrapping her legs around his waist. She starts giving Lee the most passionate tonguing kiss he had had in a very long time. As they kissed Lee began to maneuver them toward the cutting table; however, Kiki came out from the back stock room. Upon seeing Kiki he almost dropped Sarah. Blushing Lee says, "…didn't realize you were still here" to Kiki.

"Obviously…" Kiki says bluntly.

Then she turns to Sarah and says, "…We have to finish our conversation" also in a blunt tone. And Sarah just turned to her and says "…no I think we're done I'll talk to Lee about it" they could hear Kiki leaving as she drives away. Sarah explained that a group had been messing around with some of the smaller growers fields and their grow houses; sugar in generators and cutting water lines.

Lee looked at her and says "…but no, the reason you want to talk to me …there is something else".

Sarah explained that some of the group had broke into one of Derrick's orchid hot-houses and done some damage. For the most part Lee knew that there had been this uneasy truce between the loggers and growers. Lee had kept out of minor troubles between the group – figuring they could straighten it out between them selves – but he hadn't seen any trouble in town.

Lee says if the trouble got worse just to let him know. "Then… that small purplish orchid I was carrying, the one that had a perfume like smell, had it come from Derrick's place?" Lee says as he looks sternly at Sarah.

"Yeah, Kiki brought over the orchid that were in the hothouse that the group broke into; some were Derrick's special orchids and hard to come by" Sarah responded.

"Then you'll answer the calls if one of the small growers calls you about some damage" Sarah quickly says as she took Lee's hand. "Tell Derrick that he can call me anytime but not anyone else; Donnie has too much on his plate right now to get him involved" .

Lee quickly responds as he looks into Sarah's eyes. "Is your son part of the group that we chased out of town some months back; after they got rowdy with a couple of growers and the barmaid" Lee asked concerned that the trouble had gotten down to Barber.

"Yeah, he told me how he was glad you didn't recognize him…Why" Sarah says concerned that her son is involved in the trouble. "I just want to make sure that your boy stays away from certain groups that journey down to Barber."

Lee finally gets to the conversation that he wants to have with Sarah and says, "The evidence orchid I showed you….".

"The one that is such a secret…." Sarah quickly responds.

"Yeah…." Lee answers and continues "One of the orchids that I helped you and Kiki with had the same or similar smell as my evidence orchid. Where did those orchids come from?"

"From Derrick's green house we were rescuing them from the fire" Sarah responds.

"What was the name of the orchid, again?" Lee gently asks Sarah.

"A Gongora" Sarah replies

"… and is the orchid rare or fairly common?" Lee continues in a more inter-rogation style. "Its very rare found in only one area in South America. Why…?"

"Just curious, that's all…." Lee responds.

"You don't think that Derrick had anything to do with your case" Sarah asked nervously.

"I don't know, just trying to fit together the pieces" Lee replied in a matter of fact manner so as to end the conversation… and kissed Sarah good-bye and gave an excuse that Donnie would be wondering where he was…

CHAPTER 11

THE BARTLETS AND JUAN

Lee pulls his cruiser in front of the motel, the morning mist still hung softly in the air.

As he walks into the check-in office, he is immediately greeted with a hardy "Good Morning Lee come for some coffee and pastry?…We don't usually see you over here this early…something I can do for you?" the motel owner inquires. Lee asks if he'd seen Ed Falconer up and about… that he sees his Limo is still in the parking lot. "Oh they left early in one of Tom's 4X4 rentals …says they are off to check out the coastal redwoods and headed out just about sun-up" is the response. Lee thought he will not underestimate Ed again and has that feeling of being behind the eight ball and late for the party all at once. Lee grabs his cell phone from his cruiser and walks across the street to <u>Tom's USED CARS & Rentals</u>.

Tom is the town's local preacher and used car dealer an odd combination but it works well for Tom who has been in Barber since before the '72 flood. Tom is out washing off the morning mist from his used cars. "You're out early …expecting a rush on your used car sales"? Lee says with a half chuckle. Tom smiles back …"some city guy and his driver came here early, wanting to get and early start for a tour of the Redwoods and the Coastal Mountains. They called me last night to make sure I had a four wheel drive vehicle; then they took one of my best;

sure a lot more vehicle than what they need". Lee thanks Tom and asks if they had maps of the area "Yeah they said they had mapped it out last night … they seem to know where they were going" Tom responded. The sickening feelings that he had missed this one stopped Lee cold. Lee asked if Tom knows where they might be headed as Lee takes out his cell phone.

Lee calls up to Eureka to see if they have found out anything about their John Doe …it has been awhile since they had called with any official information. Lee listened as the Sheriff explained that they had identified some dirt and mud on the body's pants, as coming from the Coastal Mountain areas and that is not from the area and that's all they knew. Lee gave them the information about the John Doe's probable information and suggested that they might be calling on them to ID the body. Lee got into his cruiser and headed back to the station.

Lee goes straight back to the substation to his desk. As he reaches for the phone Donnie hovered around Lee's desk as Lee thumbed through his Rolodex looking for a number. Lee began to feel that cramped feeling of too many people in the room, and says "Donnie, our coffee is tasting a little bitter, and I didn't have a chance to stop by Marge's; would you go down to the Café and get us some of Marge's special blend and some kind of pastry for us both?". Lee reached into the desk drawer and pulled out some dollar bills and continues looking in the Rolodex as he handed the dollars to Donnie. Now Lee had rarely asked Donnie to go get anything – and Donnie could tell that he isn't invited to join in on what-ever conversation is going to take place.

Donnie took the money and repeated the instructions back to Lee in a voice that Sally at the Café would of used "…that is coffee – special blend and some pastry – for us both". Lee just nods his head acknowledging the order and that Donnie is not particularly pleased about the request.

Lee picks up the phone receiver immediately punches in some numbers "Sarah … do you know anything about your Ex being in town…?" There is a pause that made Lee uncomfortable.

"Kyle called me last night to let me know that his father is in town… Kyle wouldn't or didn't say why he is here …". Sarah response,

"Well I'm looking at this card that he gave to Donnie yesterday ... he stayed at the motel last night..." Lee responds flatly trying not to show that he is irritated that she hadn't said anything yesterday.

"Lee ..." Sarah responds sharply "...I just found out last night";

Lee says, "OK...ok..." and hung up the phone less than pleased at Sarah's response. Lee glances at the County Sherriff's phone number and shook his head "...how'd they come to that conclusion...Coastal Mountain dirt?". Scratched his head and thought ' ...and they didn't believe that the John Doe came from the area ...like maybe a drug deal gone really bad...?. Lee thought as he could hear Donnie's heavy footsteps hitting the wooden sidewalk – he could tell that Donnie is quick stepping it.

Donnie quickly opens the door and yells over to Lee "...THEY'RE gone.... the guy's from that Pharmacy company" Donnie is breathing hard and Lee could see that Donnie is upset and didn't have any coffee.

Donnie quickly says, "I stopped over at the motel to see if that guy from the Pharmacy Company is at the motel and they said he left early. Like sunrise with one of Tom's rental 4 bys...paid for the night and says they would be staying a few more nights...then drove out heading toward the coast ...says something about wanting to see some 'Ancient Redwoods' along the coast...but they're aren't many tall redwoods out that way ...just old Costal Cedars. ...Right?" Donnie is letting his excitement get the better of him and Lee just smiles not wanting to spoil Donnie's moment and that he already knew. Lee smiles and shakes his head as he reaches for the phone and motioned for Donnie to sit down; then put his finger to his lips – and Donnie tried to quiet his heavy breathing.

Donnie gets up quickly and comes back with a note and hands it to Lee as he recognized that Lee is talking to one of the Bartley's' that live in the coastal mountains along one of the old dirt roads off the main road. Lee read Donnie's note as he talked to the Bartley older son...and looked inquisitively at Donnie; the note just read 'Juan – knows' and Lee shrugged his shoulder at Donnie.

Donnie tried to patiently listen as Lee talked to the Bartley boy. "So there was some kind of car accident off the King's Peak road ...but you don't know if anyone is hurt…you just heard about a car being pulled out of one of the steep ravines off of King's Road…OK…Thank you for the information… I'll call you back later after I look into it." Lee hung up the phone and allows Donnie to say what is obviously going to be his investigation find. "Juan says that there is some kind of car accident off of Kings Road the night before they found the body at the Park entrance; but that it is all hushed up REAL QUIET like and no one is supposed to talk about it."

Lee punched in numbers on his cell phone while Donnie looked with a puzzled expression. "Call me back when you can…" is all Lee says in the phone then looked at Donnie and says, "…Feel like a ride? But we may not be back until late…?"

Donnie paused and Lee felt that is a good sign; he smiled at Donnie and says "…it will be ok just going looking for some information, someone has to follow-up on what Juan knows …or, thinks he knows…?" Donnie looks at Lee and just knew that meant he is going on to the next level – which he honestly didn't think he really wanted to know at all. Donnie felt protected in not knowing, just hearing about what really went on in Emerald.

Donnie knew that underneath Emerald's beauty lay a whole nether world …an underground economy that is to be respected and not to be taken lightly. "If you think you need me …I'm there …but I got to tell you that although my young mind says yes…my older mind says not so fast and take it slow…" Donnie responds with a calm expression that Lee is glad to see. "Come on …we'll take it slow" and Lee shot back a mentors grin; with a wink that made Donnie feel better inside.

Lee's cell phone rang "Thanks" is all Lee says and put the phone in his inside jacket pocket.

Donnie follows Lee close behind and says "maybe I better stay never know what is going to happen and I can talk to Juan."

"Oh come on you can show off to me your investigation skills". Lee responds.

Lee is quiet as he bumped along the rough road and didn't offer much in the way of conversation excepted to ask how Donnie is doing in dating Sally. It is common talk around town that Donnie and Sally are an item; and Donnie liked that for he knew people would respect his feelings and all other interested men would back off. Everyone knows Emerald is a stake your claim man, women, land, water wells, whatever: if people thought you had laid a claim no one is going to put up a fuss unless there needs to be one. A lot of men had asked Sally out but when Donnie walked her to the grocery store that pretty much did it – Sally and Donnie were an item. Most people in town were glad to see it.

As they start the series of sharp mountain curves climbing through the steep mountain roadway, there is only one lane at times. Lee could sense that Donnie had tightened up – griping the steering wheel too tight for the road. Lee asked Donnie if he knew Sarah. Donnie had heard in town that Lee is spending a lot of time over in Fortuna – and had heard Sarah was once part of the original group of people that had started a commune and helped build up Emerald – but that she had left and no one says why or talked about it – It is just the way people were in Emerald '…Live and let Live…'. Donnie feels a good surprise when Lee asks – for Lee is never one for talking about his personal life. Donnie smiles and relaxes his grip on the steering wheel.

"No – Oh I know of her and what people talk about – her being part of the original group of people to get things started in Emerald" Donnie responds politely; that she left for a time and is back living in Northern Emerald." Lee feels more comfortable as Donnie relaxes his grip on the steering wheel and is easier on the steep turns.

Lee sits back and relaxes in his seat and says in a matter fact tone "…I'm thinking of asking her out again – going to some nice place up North, one of the restaurants up there – so there won't be all the talk to deal with in town".

Donnie just grinned "…. maybe you should think about taking her to the movie here in town and go to 'Charles' for diner – you know it might just quiet all that talk and slow down all the women that have been trying to get to know you better". Donnie replies with a confident chuckle in his voice. Donnie felt relaxed and real good that they are having a real conversation.

Lee just responds with a "Huh..!" and had a smile on his face. It is just after that that Lee says, "...Turn on to Kings Road...it is coming up in a few more miles". Donnie's mind began to race trying to figure out where they would be going – maybe to see where that car had driven off the road – and decides not to ask a question that he had already asked.

"I thought we might drop in to see Derrick" Lee says in a matter of fact way so as not to make Donnie nervous – and is glad they were on a level stretch of the road. Donnie didn't know the roads in the backcountry – Lee had been taking care of all the calls that involved the backcountry. Donnie tried to relax but is growing concerned about what they would be doing, going to Derrick's place – and what that had to do with what they were doing. Then Donnie realized who Lee is talking to on the cell phone before and now he had a sinking feel that this had to do with that man from that pharmacy company.

"Think we might run into that guy from the Pharmacy Company out here?" Donnie asked trying to imply that he is listening and thinking about what Lee had said.

Lee just says "...maybe so.." in a quiet voice. Donnie's mind is racing – and he wished that they were talking about Sarah or Sally.

Lee says, "...The turn out to King Road is just up ahead to the right.... Take it easy on the road, it's part dirt and part paving that is need of repair". Donnie is feeling like he would rather be the passenger on this trip but counted on Lee knowing exactly what he is doing. The entrance to King Road is all Lee had said Donnie had encountered these kinds of roads before but Lee had always told him to come back because he didn't want to have to ask to have the cruiser repaired.

"I need to talk to Derrick about the accident and see if we run into that guy from the Pharmacy Company" Lee responds to Donnie's puzzled expression. As Donnie tried to negotiate the rough terrain of the road and listen to Lee - they suddenly hit a pothole hard and they both bounced up against the seat belts of their seats; "Whoa...partner...I better take over from here ...this road can be tricky" Lee says responding to the pothole.

Donnie immediately pulled the cruiser to a stop, seeming thankful that Lee had made the suggestion; the long trip is beginning to wear on him. Lee got out to switch sides with Donnie as he jokes with Donnie about his driving. The mountain air on the ridgeline is cool with the ocean breeze and it feels good to stretch his legs; Donnie gets out and they both enjoyed a break. They were on top the ridgeline where you could see for miles in all directions where the scars of past clear cutting stood out – but you could also see the tops of 'the Ancients' those tall of the tallest redwoods that had been spared, as a compromise that the lumber companies could cut patches around the great trees. Donnie hears the blades of a large helicopter swooshing against cool air off some distance away and large tree log dangled in the air several 100 feet above from its cable like so much meat to slaughter. Donnie remarks at how the logging industry had changed and at least they weren't cutting roads into the forest anymore. The Barber radio station called about the logging helicopter that came in scratching over the car radio and Donnie laughed – Lee thought it is good to see that Donnie understands it all.

They talk a while about the changes that had been forced to occur in logging and how the logging companies kept up with the change through technology. Lee remarked "…its all just a balance everyone seems to understand that …at least… they may not like it but …they all know they have to find a balance…".

Donnie asks if Lee thought that there would be a balance in the marijuana growing.

Lee remarked "…it's coming …and then more change will be forced on Emerald". Lee took the opportunity to call in to the station to make sure that everything is ok in town; of course if it isn't, there isn't much that they can do being so far out – but it did help the town folks to know that he is checking in. Lee smiles at Donnie and says "Tom must know we're gone he's smelting glass in his furnace and Marge has been over to talk to him."

Donnie says "it doesn't change much does it…at least everyone seems to solve their own troubles where they can" Lee nods in acknowledgement and they both got back in to the cruiser. Donnie looks over to Lee as he fastens himself in and started up the cruise "seems like we'd seen that pharmacy's guy – by now - with all the distance we could see from this ridge-road…";

Lee looked over and smiled and says …"maybe" so…Donnie…maybe so".

Donnie sits back into the seat satisfied with the answers and that he is beginning to formulate what is going on in his head – but is having a problem with some missing piece.

Lee glances and looks at Donnie as he turns-on the cruiser's four-wheel drive …" it's likely Mr. Falconer came here to see his son as well as looking for his dead employee".

"Whose his son…do you know him?" Donnie says inquisitively.

"Kyle." Lee responds with sternest to his voice. Donnie thought that is something to think about and sat-up as Lee maneuvered around the ruts and potholes in the road.

CHAPTER 12

ED AND KYLE

Ed and his driver are heading down the Pleasant Pike through the steep downhill grade, one lane road, which you could almost call a road. It is obvious that Ed's driver should stick to Limo driving – he had originally told Ed to find someone but Ed let his pocket book do the talking and the driver is glad to oblige him. The driver grips the steering wheel as it tugged at his hands; "…are you sure that there will be someone to take me back to my Limo today?" the driver says nervously to Ed.

"YES…. YES just watch those ruts", the steering wheel jerked so hard that it threw the drivers hand temporarily off the steering wheel. "Watch it…" Ed yells at the driver. As they pull down the grade to a flat meadow pasture with a few steers grazing – seeming to not give a second thought to the intruders. Ed yells "STOP here … let's give it a rest" just as they are pulling off the dirt road, a large modified 4x4 truck comes out from the forest behind the lock bar gate. It sits high with enormous black tires – the truck looks as though it had seen lots of the muddy forbidding dirt and rough roads. A man jumps out of the truck next to the driver and is standing with a large rifle pointed towards them. Ed quickly put up his hands and yells at his driver to do the same. The truck pulls in close, pointing straight at the jeeps side – it is obvious that Ed and his driver weren't going to be going anywhere. Ed rolls down the side window and yells "…we're here to see Kyle - my son…" in a half stern half very concerned voice. "Who are you … and what do you want with Kyle…?" the man with the gun says angrily; and continues to point what they now see as a 30 odd 6 shot gun – that at this distance would cut them in half. "Would you please just call Kyle …he is expecting me…?" Ed says in the best calming voice that he could muster; for Ed rarely if ever says 'please' to anyone.

The man with the shotgun nods to the driver who picks up a cell phone and talks softly into it…. The driver looks back at the man with the shotgun, and the gun is lowered; but not the look of suspicion that now permeates the air. The gunman continues his stare; but Ed feels the relief of some type of recognition is to be had …no matter how sinister the look. Ed thought they better not make any sudden moves – but he could feel the cold damp air in his bones and his heavy jacket is a dangerous grab away in the 4x4.

Suddenly the sound of a large engine vehicle could be heard coming through the forest from behind the locked bar gate pole on the other muddy dirt road in the forest. The driver beside the gunman jumps from the truck and quickly steps to the gate – unlocks it and swings the bar open for access to the road. Kyle's truck roared out of the forest sounding like some enormous tractor that would be pulling a semi - a truck much larger than it is. The truck roared past the road bar-pole gate and around the vehicle that the gunman are in, and pulls in front of Ed's vehicle so to block any way out. Kyle jumped from his truck, landing hard, carrying a stern look on his face but then smiles and walks towards Ed. Ed sits frozen – not sure what is about to happen, Ed barely recognizes his son who had left when he was 18 – from any of the photos that Kyle had sent to him, but he did look every bit a man in his late 30's. Kyle is larger and bigger than he expects and looks as though he had been on some trek deep in the woods for months.

Ed exits the vehicle as they approach each other cautiously. "Hey, fellers this here is my old man …he may look thin …but he's made of tough meat…I should know" Kyle yelled out while looking into Ed's eyes. Ed managed a smile – that would crack his face – and waved to the gunman; that now had at least lowered his rifle.

"What the fuck are you doing here why didn't you let me know? Now let's go get something to eat" Kyle says in a friendly but cautious voice.

"I got to get my driver back to his vehicle and on his way" Ed says not moving from their jeep.

"The trouble is …DAD…he knows where I live and that is not a good thing… he's family" Kyle says as he turns back towards Ed. Kyle cracked a wide smile and says "just kidding…Frank here will take him back" although Ed thought there might be some truth to his statement.

The driver looks nervously at Ed and says "that will be fine with me Mr. Falconer… I really got to be getting Tom's jeep…back to him and…. the sheriff will be expecting us back after our outing in the woods.

"Kyle turns his attention back to Ed's driver; as the driver says nervously "…. oh the sheriff doesn't know where…we are…but".

"Oh you mean Lee…?" Kyle says quickly cutting the driver off from saying anything further. "Lee and I are good friends and I'll have one of the boys take the jeep and you back to Tom's" Kyle says with a grimness smile.

Frank motions to Ed's driver and says, "Come on before it gets much colder".

And Ed responds, "Thanks for all your help" and Ed walks over to the driver and hands him a roll of bills. Ed says just under his breath "…it'll be fine. This is my son…you'll be fine". Frank and the driver leave and they all load up in the trucks and head off to Kyle's cabin.

CHAPTER 13
AKIKO

As Kyle walks through his doorway, Ed thinks to himself this is more a cabin than a home. Kyle says to Ed "Frank will make sure that your driver gets back to town safely…that is unless you don't want him to…"Kyle says with a chuckle. "No…NO…no I mean" Kyle cut him off in mid-sentence "…relax it is a joke". Just in time to break the silence, a beautiful young raven haired woman seeming to be in her mid 20's walked in from the kitchen.

Ed is taken back "…I'd like for you to meet Kiki, she works over at mom's shop in Fortuna…" Kyle says looking at Kiki. Ed is struck by her tall thin stature and obviously of some Asian background.

Ed says as he regained his composure - "So nice to meet you; you work at Sarah shop in Fortuna?".

"That's the only one around" she says with a polite smile; for she knew that look that Ed had on his face. "You look like you could do with some rest from that city life…we can always tell folks that are from the city…let me get you boys some beers" Kiki says returning Ed's look with only the slightness of flirting. Ed's gaze follows Kiki as she disappeared into the kitchen .

"…She's taken…Pops…" Kyle says with a chuckle. "I called my boss Ron… figured that we'd have some lunch, maybe make a stop at Ron's local place and have some pizza, before we head out" Kyle says as Kiki comes back with cold beer and a joint.

"Is that wise…?" Ed says and stops as Kyle gave him a smirk of a grin.

"Don't mind Kiki she's just part of the gang; if it weren't for Kiki I'd been busted long ago" Kyle says, watching as Kiki left for the kitchen; "…pretty to watch…huh…pop's" Kyle continues. "She's part of the network community that keeps us safe with information she get's from the Sheriff station" Kyle says with a belch of beer.

Kiki came back in the living room with her coat on and Ed immediately stood up "…that's sweet… you can tell he is from Texas…not like some…"Kiki says finishing putting on her coat. "I got to be off…going to work; be at Sarah's; she's will be waiting… you come by sometime …you promised" Kiki says as she gives Kyle a kiss; "…and don't worry about opening the door…" she says looking at Kyle.

✳ ✳ ✳ ✳ ✳

Donnie and Lee bounce along the mountain road slipping some in the mud, dodging ruts and rocks that had broken off from the mountain hillside. Donnie is struck with the beauty of the area, you could see for miles and you could also see that there isn't going to be clear skies before long; "…looks like rain coming our way; sure hope we can get out before any rains comes in…" Donnie laments – trying to fill in the dead air in the conversation. Lee gave a smile as he stared straight at the road ahead; and adjusted himself in the seat. Before long Lee turns on to a road that is gentler by Emerald standards; Donnie could see they are heading into the forest – it seems to take control of everything and the road is filled with shadows and grew a little darker because of it.

Lee takes another turn on to a road; and although it is a dirt road it obviously has been graded and Donnie is grateful not to be bouncing against his seat belt. Suddenly there is an asphalt roadway just smooth as it could be, no markings on the road but it sure is black; Donnie's heart began to race just a bit as he felt his nerves get the better of him. They drove on the asphalt roadway for a while – all-along the forest closing in closer and closer. Donnie could see the area is posted with old beat-up metal NO TREASSPASING signs that were nailed on old barbwire fences and on large trees – the signs looked almost natural to the area, like you would expect them to be there.

Lee comes to a stop in front of a large metal 12 foot gate – that looked out of place, like it belonged on some big estate, only not so ornate – as some of the bigger cattle ranchers had. Lee stops and gets out the 4x4 cruiser and walks over to Donnie's side and into the forest about 10 feet, stops and begins talking into cell phone that Donnie had not seen before. After a minute or so he walks back out of the forest on to the well-worn pathway; and got back into the cruiser. They sit for a minute or so – and then Lee slowly shakes his head and waved his hands in the air – as if to say 'well are you going to open up or not'? And the large gate swung open. Donnie says, "…What is that all about…" Lee just shakes his head and shrugs his shoulders.

They drove on the smooth asphalt roadbed for about a mile – with Donnie taking it all in nervously – trying not to ask questions – he knew now the questions would keep until they started back – whenever that would be. Then the asphalt roadway turns up a slight hill. As they clear the hill, there it is, the most beautiful old farmhouse that Donnie has ever seen. There is an old three foot stone wall that lead up to the house on either side of the driveway; the siding of the house is wood and painted an old blue-gray neat with trimming; and there is a farm porch that wraps all along the front of the house and seems to continue on around on the sides. The whole of the front area of the house is well maintained and there is a large pond below the house on Lee's side.

They pull up and park the cruiser on the stone gravel area next to an old white painted out-building. The fire at the greenhouse had been all cleaned up; the only thing that remained was the acrid smell of old burning wood. Lee looks over at Donnie and gets out of the cruiser and Donnie although not sure, got out as well. On the porch is a man medium built with a graying, closely cut beard neatly trimmed, dressed in denim and an all to comfortable flannel shirt. Next to him is a beautiful Asian looking woman with long dark raven hair about the same age dressed in a long comfortable printed dress, with her hair up but with strands of her hair that had gotten away from her head. Donnie, with Lee in front of him walk on the gravel path that leads to the wooden stairs in front to the porch. Donnie admired the greenery around the house and imagined that spring must be a beautiful picture except for the burned out greenhouse.

The man smiles at Lee and extends his hand and says, "…Lee, you didn't tell me that we are going to have company…" with a grin; and with that the man extended his hand to Donnie and says, "I'm Derrick and this is Akiko" looking over to the beautiful older woman. Donnie thought he almost immediately felt comfortable, this isn't at all what he had expected, although he didn't know quite what he expected this had to be a business call or something.

Akiko opened the white screen door that creaks as she opened it and says, "…. welcome to our home, kick off your boots…Maria is not fond of cleaning up mud". Donnie looks down at his muddy boots; then sees Lee unlace his boots at the doorstep and remove his boots; Donnie felt relieved and followed suit.

The door opens directly in to the living room, which is warmly decorated in a style, reminiscent of the old Victorian era with fine wood furnishings. Donnie is struck with the feeling of warmth and hominess in the room; and that it all must of cost a pretty penny. He nervously glanced around and followed Lee to a large dark blue sofa towards the back of the room; with large bay windows that looked out to the valley to the East. Derrick joked that it is difficult to find an opportunity to use the large living room. They loved decorating it and it did not get the use that they had hoped for – people felt uncomfortable as if it is too formal.

"Well it sure has nice furniture, the dark blues and reds just make it lovely" Donnie remarks.

"You didn't tell me your deputy is a decorator …Lee" Akiko chuckled to the group as Donnie blushed.

"So what brings you out our way?" Derrick says casually as he sat down in a well-upholstered straight back chair. Derrick seems in a get down to business tone.

Lee turned to Derrick and says "I'd like to discuss the fire here at your place and know if you know anything about the rental car that drove off the embankment on the Mt. Drake Road". Derrick casually sits back in his chair and glances over at Donnie who, is now sitting on the sofa edge and then glances over to Akiko who is casually walking toward them. "Would you all like some hot tea or maybe a hot toddy" Akiko says in a soft low voice as if she would be interrupting the group. There were polite no's from Donnie and Lee; and Derrick says, "…that would be nice – I bet you both have been hitting the old road pretty hard". "Donnie, could you to lend me a hand. I believe the tea and toddy may be about ready" Akiko says turning to Donnie. Donnie is stunned and hadn't counted on helping out.

Lee turns to Donnie and says "Don't worry you won't miss anything" Lee could see that they had been expected and Donnie's presences concerned Derrick. Donnie reluctantly got up and followed Akiko back towards the kitchen – feeling more disgruntled than he should have. Donnie and Akiko disappear behind the kitchen wall. Derrick leans forward towards Lee, and says, "…you understand… you and I have smoked a pipe but …well…" Derrick paused and Lee filled in the conversation "…yeah, but from what I hear you and I have a lot to talk about". Derrick sat back in his chair and says "..You and I have always been honest with one another…and that has not changed…has it?"

"No it hasn't …" Lee responds sitting back in his chair.

Derrick told how he knew that the car that went off the road is just an accident. It is an unfortunate accident…?". Lee ask, "Do you know who was… driving the car?" in a somewhat friendly but irritated low voice. Derrick purses his lip

"…you know - it is that guy that you found dead… over by the park entrance… that is what I hear Derricks say".

Lee gave his head a slight turn and with some irritation looked directly into Derrick's eyes. "WHY THE HELL…didn't you tell me this before? Did the fire have anything to do with all this? How are you both?" Lee asked in an irritated low voice.

"Lee you know me, I don't get involved in police business that does not concern me…and I'm sure as hell not going to get involved in something …THAT IS someone else's business," Derrick firmly responds. Lee knew Derrick long enough to know it is true …but at least he could get some information.

Derrick explains that he thought, "that the fire was not an accident but he has it covered, there is no need for his help". He continues…"The accident is that the guy from Quantex that I had met at the Amsterdam CUP. Michael was coming out here to see me; and when he didn't show…and then there was the accident. I know one thing for sure silence – don't come cheap…. someone laid out some cash to make that happen…" Derrick whispers to Lee. Now Lee shows his concern about where this is all heading.

Derrick could read Lee's concern and responds; "…but the whole thing was an accident …there is nothing in this – it is just an accident…".

"Explain how a dead guy ends up perched on the park Granite marker…and you say it is an accident" Lee says in a truly irritated whisper. Derrick explains how he had heard it is Kyle and Frank that messed up some job …that Kyle and Frank were supposed to intercept this guy Michael …before he got up this far…. and they just screwed it all up.

Akiko and Donnie came in "…got your tea and cookies" Donnie says in a very sarcastic voice. Lee and Derrick helped themselves and Akiko looks over at the fireplace, which is growing low. Akiko turns to Donnie as he began to sit down "Donnie…would you give me a hand with some firewood from the back shed…" Donnie could sense what is going on and smiles politely with a stare at Lee.

"That deputy of yours catches on quick…smart fellow…" Derrick says softly to Lee as Donnie and Akiko head out the door. "Yeah, just when we were beginning to bond and …I know this is going to cost me" Lee responded with a grin. Derrick went on to explain that Michael had talked about "…. a relationship with Quantex …that would benefit everyone…" and that Michael was coming out to talk. That he had no idea that anyone even knew who he was. …Let alone try to intercept him." Derrick continues, but explains that there is only one person that "…would have that much information. …AND try to intercept Michael".

Lee looks at Derrick with some disbelief and frustration. Derrick explains that Ron and he are after the same thing; he just did not think Ron would go to such extremes…. He probably has something to do with the fire here – but don't you pay it any mind it will be taken care of. "…But all things considered it is the dead guy was just an accident…" as far as he knew.

Lee probes Derrick for some answers "…so what is this really all about…?" But Derrick dodges them in a way that had kept he and family safe all these years.

"You know Kyle's father came out for a visit…" Lee says trying to see if he could get a reaction from Derrick that would tell him more about what is going on. "I'm sure it's not really to see Kyle or Sarah" Derrick responds with the grimmest of looks. With that remark Derrick had just given him all the information that he is going to get and Lee responds gratefully

"…Thanks Derrick…. I guess I need to see after Sarah"; Derrick says.

"No problem …but you don't need to worry about Sarah" and with that Lee knew that they had finished their business and it is time to leave. Lee gives Derrick a warm heart felt hand shake and says, "Thanks just the same…"

Lee and Derrick sit and drink some tea and waited for Donnie and Akiko to get back and talk of how things had changed and his trip to Amsterdam.

✳   ✳   ✳   ✳   ✳

Ed sits a little nervous not knowing what is going to happen – he knows he didn't feel like the game of catch – not that he ever did much of that. "So what have you been up to…?" Ed says looking at Kyle.

"I'm good, don't need any money, and life has been pretty good – got a place… Thanks to you…and money is coming in the door …like I told you it would". Ed clinks beer bottles with his son, and wants to get going but didn't want to seem rude.

"Look, why don't we eat in the truck on the way over"; Kyle says seeing his father's nervousness; Ed smiles and appreciates that Kyle could read him without drawing an awkward situation out.

"Yep…looks like you are doing real good…" Ed says as he looks around half in earnest.

Kyle spoke a little about his plans to move up north …"…cause you know I'm not one for crowds…and I need to be doing my own thing". "…. Hmm"

Ed responds adding "…don't like crowds…going to do your own thing. …I believe the part about doing your own thing …but not liking crowds…?" Ed gave Kyle a sideways look.

"Yeah …like you always told me 'know the size of your pond" Kyle responds with a half chuckle. Ed tries to make some small talk about Akiko…(Kiki mother) and whether she knew about her plans. "She's all right; but she has a real thing about money…not sure that is going to work…'no expectations' you know pop and they headed out to the truck.

CHAPTER 14

PURPLE

Ed and Kyle bounce on the road out of Pleasanton "someone should do something about this road" Ed says almost having to shout over the roar of Kyle's truck engine. "…. Its not mine to worry about …that's the way we like it…" Kyle responded in a matter fact way …and Ed had a sense of the real meaning.

A slight mist is moving in as they head out of Pleasanton on to the Pike road that would take them to Barber. The road is smoother now that they are on the asphalt and Ed thought now is the time he better get his conversation out how and WHY Michael had died. "So what happened…?" Ed bluntly says to Kyle in his corporate tone; and Kyle knew what the real question was. "It was an accident… that's all …just an accident…you know shit happens out here" Kyle responds with a straight face staring out at the road.

"You connected to it …or have any troubles?" Ed probes. Kyle quickly responds, "Like …I said…it was an accident…that's all you need to know…. and that is probably too much…. So don't ask. …And I won't have to tell. I'm fine …as long no one says anything…". Ed sat back and let his thoughts take him over all that he had lost in Sarah and Kyle. Ed sat back and enjoys the scenery as it went by. Kyle says, "see, the rental car is gone …like I said I would take care of it". "Is Tom going to get his rental back?" Ed asked as Kyle smiles and stares out at the road "..You don't have to worry dad…it's all good…" Ed decides that he has all the information that he is going to get and decides to join Kyle in small talk. But Kyle had become a person of Emerald and didn't care for small talk – not that he is any good at it – he just never sees the need for it.

Kyle reaches over toward Ed – and banged his fist against the glove compartment, Kyle quips "Why don't you light us up one and sit back an enjoyed the scenery".

Ed reaches into the glove compartment and pulled a pint size baggie; with Purplish marijuana buds and several rolled joints. Kyle chuckled and says, "Don't never know when you are going to need a smoke" and pulls out his butane lighter. Kyle flicks the lighter and a small blue gas flame shot out of it. Ed took Kyle response to mean that is the end of conversation and pulled out two joints.

As Ed sucked and drew in the smoke …he recalled that it had been awhile. The weed is as strong as he had hoped, and knew too much is going to be no good, so he decides to try not to inhale but feels it is as good as what Michael had. Kyle drew in the smoke and tried his smoke ring trick to show off; Ed enjoyed the effort and enjoyed the peace of mind that the weed offers to him.

There isn't a lot of conversation after Ed and Kyle had lit the joint and enjoyed the peace of a drive through some beautiful country. As they pass the half way-point, Kyle turned to his Dad to see how he is doing with the weed. Ed stares at the country going by. Kyle says. "…So you plan to see Mom while you up here?"

Ed is almost too stoned to respond. Ed's thoughts drift to Sarah and how they had met, her smiling face began to take over his every memory – felt possessed and shock - his head trying to snap out of where he is and between a few coughs Ed responded, "…don't know yet…and did you grow this stuff?".

Kyle laughs and says "..Why spend the effort growing it when it's yours for the taking" and adds "you know she has a flower and rock shop up north in Fortuna…she looks good…kind of at peace with it all…it might be a good thing". Ed stares out the widow and watches the beautiful countryside go by and after some minutes says "wherever you got this …its very good stuff…you get it from Ron"?

Kyle drives as the trees speed by at 60 MPH on the old road. When they get further in the forest and start the climb out of the coastal mountains, Kyle says "…Ron couldn't grow this…and you watch out for any deals you make with Ron…he didn't get where he is without breaking a few things you know bones and stuff…and don't get on his bad side… things could go very bad". And after a few sharp turns they were out on the way. Kyle adds, "…that's all I'm say-in". Ed is still lost in where the weed had come from; it isn't the normal grass high he had expected but much more with a psychedelic feel to it like Michael's stuff.

Before Ed knew what he is saying, "this is Derrick & Paul's isn't it… How'd you get it…?" Ed knew the answer even if Kyle didn't tell him;

Kyle responded as the road smoothed out ahead "…I don't think its Derrick and Paul anymore …just Derrick…and Ron with his money." Ed didn't quite get where Kyle is coming from but knew that after he came out of this haze he is in – but he'd figure it all out – he always did.

The road dumps out into a smooth asphalt, with fog lined white and yellow painted centerline as they got nearer to Barber. Ed notices neat small old houses some with lawn, others with cars parked where the lawn should be. Most of the houses looked kept-up, some even with white picket fences, and everywhere tall 100-foot redwoods. Ed thought how quaint the neighborhood looked, peaceful, no hustle and bustle; with large blackberry bushes in the vacant lots. He is enjoying the beauty of it all when he realizes that this is a town. "I thought we were going to see Ron. Where are we going…?" Ed complained.

"You're hungry aren't you?" Kyle's asked. Ed thought, not such a bad idea as he felt the munchies coming on. They wound through a neighborhood on to a side road, and Ed sees a restaurant coming towards them like any other restaurant diner. Kyle drove past the front of the restaurant, and pulled around back of where older beat-up vehicles were parked. Kyle says, "it's Pizza and Italian food – did you see the sign?" As he chuckled softly. Kyle pulls up next to the kitchen door. "You go on in I got to go and pick up Frank…"

Ed opened the door in a robot like motion. Ed isn't quite sure of what to make of this change in plans "but I don't know anyone here" Ed states.

Kyle looked perturbed and says; "look I'll be right back; you don't need to know anyone – everyone already knows you; besides its Ron's place" and laughs.

Ed walks into the kitchen – as instructed and everyone in the kitchen gave that look 'like what are you doing here' but no one says a word. One of the cooks gives a nod toward an open hallway and Ed sees a server with a pizza platter coming towards him. He quickly walks down the red walled paper short hallway and into the restaurant. The restaurant looks like it could seat near a hundred people and is half filled with people in jeans and shirts. Ed thought nothing out the ordinary. A waiter came over to him and says "sit where you want" and Ed walked to a table meant for four people near the window. He looked up at the waiter and says, "there are some people coming to join me" the waiter lays down a menu and walks away.

Ed tries not to be self-conscience, as he looks around at all the old metal beer and hard liquor signs that adorned the wall; he notices people's glances. Ed thinks his clothes perhaps look too new – compare to everyone there; but he puts on a pleasant smile and pickups the menu. The waiter came by and Ed ordered coffee he says, "While I wait for the others" and that seems to satisfy the waiter.

Twenty minutes pass and the waiter comes over looking frustrated, and says, "Are your friends from around here?".

Ed is getting concerned and responds, "Yes my son, Kyle and his friend, I believe he said his name is Frank". The waiter smiles and says "it's not likely they'd be coming here" and looked down at Ed. Ed is now perplexed, but he didn't want to ask questions, and says, "Well then, is Ron about" the waiter smiled and acknowledge

Ed like maybe Ed is OK and says "Nah, he's probably in Redwood Glenn at his fancy place. Why, is he supposed to join you?". Ed put on his best corporate face and says, "Would you give him a call and tell him I'm here".

It seems to have worked for the waiter who says, "sure" and is off toward the kitchen. A few minutes past and the waiter returns and says, "he's sending a car around for you – should be here in twenty minutes – or so" and asks if he wants anything and then says, "Ron says that whatever you want is on the house – no charge". Ed looked at the menu and ordered a small Italian sub.

As the minutes go by, Ed stares out at the misty rain and the tall redwoods that dot the sides of the front parking area. He thought this looked so normal, not like he'd imagined – just a quaint small town. Ed is losing himself in thoughts of Sarah and how she had stormed out of his ranch house 'I can't breathe here – I need to be near the ocean or at least some redwoods.' He could see what she is yelling about. The restaurant door opens and Ed notices the restaurant seem quieter; a large man steps through the door into the restaurant after leaving his large black SUV in front of the restaurant entrance.

The large man walks over to Ed's table and says, "I'm Stephen, I'm here to drive you to the Redwood Glenn restaurant"; and then he stood waiting for Ed to stand up. Ed got up and realizes that it seems everyone except him knew what is going on. Ed felt the damp biting cold as he stepped out of the restaurant. Stephen has the SUV car door open and waiting for him, Ed turns and says, "Where are we going"?

"Don't worry everything will be fine" is Stephens reply.

Ed stares out the widow somewhat frustrated that he could not get a conversation started with Stephen – Stephen has a silence about him that seems to fit him well. Many miles pass in silence and then Ed sees the Emerald Bridge and realized that they were leaving Emerald and grew concerned. "You know they are waiting for me in Eureka to take care of an employee's body" Ed says rather pointedly.

Ed sees Stephen's eyes look up into the rear-view mirror "We're almost there" and then says, "Everything has been taken care of "leaving Ed cold. Ed had heard stories of Ron's investments in Redwood Glenn, a first class Hotel next to a large park with the Pike River flowing silently next to it.

True to his word, Ed sees that Stephen had pulled off the highway onto a very pleasant Hotel entrance. Stephen pulls up to the stately hotel entrance, and a valet immediately open the door. "Baggage sir" comes from the valet. Ed manages to shake his head no. Ed felt comfortable being in charge, but having no idea what is going to happen, he felt resigned to enjoy himself as perhaps a tourist would. "The hotel Captain will meet you at the top of the stairway" the valet continued and Ed looks up to see a well tailored man standing at the front entrance of the hotel doorway.

This is making Ed more comfortable. This type of treatment is what he had always been used to. As the captain opened the large Hotel door, Ed walks into the hotel entrance. He found that he is amazed and impressed with all the furnishings.

The hotel had dark mahogany wood everywhere, plush deep red carpeting and brass furnishings. There were men in dressed uniforms with white gloves. Ed thought to himself a speck of dust wouldn't stand a chance here. The captain walks slightly in front of Ed and to his right side in the old British style. The captain walks to an equally well-furnished restaurant and then stopped at the entrance to whisper something to the maître d'.

Then the maître d' turned to Ed and says, "please allow me to show you to your table...Mr. Ron will be with you momentarily". Ed walks into the restaurant where dinner is being served to a room nearly full of well-attired quests. Ed felt very under-dressed in his jeans and leather jacket as the maitre d' pulls Ed's chair out for him to be seated. Ed turns and whispers in his ear "do you have a men's clothing shop in the hotel?". "Yes sir, allow me to show you the way"; Ed followed the maitre d' and then as before, he is handed off to the hotel captain.

The men's shop is not well furnished in the GQ style that Ed is really used to. A tailor walks over to Ed; Ed explained that he had not planned to come to a dinner and needs a suit. The tailor says, "Are you Mr. Falconer?"

A little taken a back Ed responded "yes"; and the tailor says the they had taken the liberty of gathering his belonging from the motel and had his best suit pressed and hanging in the last back dressing stall. Ed is impressed with how the hotel is run and thought it shows Ron's style of doing things, as he changed into his suit.

Ed is escorted to his table, and the maitre d' says, "Mr. Ron sends his apologies and wants to inform you that he has been unavoidably detained – and that you should continue with your dinner". Ed is a little distraught and had lost his appetite; however, just when he is thinking about getting up the waiter comes by. "I believe we have you listed as a deep smooth red wine drinker of the Napa area…is that correct sir?" the waiter asks. Ed is intrigued how could he come across that information…

"Yes, no tannin and well aged…" Ed responded.

"I have taken the liberty of selecting 'Reserve' Napa Valley Cabernet Sauvignon and with it might I suggest some Russian Caviar from Georgia" the waiter responded; adding "shall I call over the saucier to taste the wine for you?". Ed thought this is over the top and that it might draw attention "…no…I prefer to let my own palette do the tasting". The waiter presented the wine and Ed is suitably pleased – being careful not to show too much expression.

After accepting the wine, the waiter decanted the wine into a fine Waterford decanter and pours Ed a glass of wine from an equally fine Waterford red wine glass that he removes from under his cart. Ed decided to wave off the glass telling the waiter he preferred a softer glass that would allow it to breathe in the aromas of the wine. The waiter showed his noticeable embarrassment and told Ed that he much agreed however the Saucier had selected the glass but he would return momentarily. It is all Ed could do to keep from chuckling at the whole affair. However, as the waiter turns away, Ed smiles and turns his head with a smirk – as in disbelief. As he turns, he notices a beautiful middle aged woman sitting alone that seemed to be enjoying the spectacle, as much as Ed is. Ed smiles and nods to the woman then impulsively motions to the empty chair that is across from him at his table. She raises her glass with a return smile and seems to want to enjoy the sight from a far. Ed raised his glass and nods to her.

When the waiter returns with the lighter softer red wine glass and began to open the bottle, Ed says, "…the woman to the right and behind me in the blue dress do you know her – or rather is she waiting for someone?". "No sir, that is her usual table she comes here from time to time, however like yourself she likes to eat later and is usually alone" the waiter replied.

Ed got up from his seat and strolled over to the woman's table; introduced himself and asked if she would like to join him.

The woman says her name is Linda; she is an Euro-Asia woman with a very slight French accent from Northern California. She is vague about the exact locale – when Ed asks she only smiles. When Ed asked her to join him all she says is "…I'd be charmed…".Ed is at the ready with Linda's chair helping her out from her table and making sure that the waiter took care of Linda's dinner needs. Additionally, it gave Ed a chance to look Linda over; she wore a moderately-tight long dark blue evening dress with a bare back and inviting neck line that hugged to her shape – Ed smiles walking behind her as the waiter shows her to her seat at Ed's table. Ed thought to himself - Linda has the appearance of a retired model, an expensive dress to be eating alone with subdued gold long earrings and small gold chain around her neck – her hair is coal black falling to her mid-back and her perfume is a wisp of "White Flowers". Ed found himself forgetting his reason for being at the restaurant in the first place as he sat down across from her. Ed's gift for conversation soon comes to his rescue – as he tries desperately to find out more about her – in Ed's usual disarming style. Ed prides himself on being able to find out about a person without the person's knowledge – it has always been his gift in his position.

Linda and Ed enjoy their appetizers and wine; a wine for Linda that Ed had of course upgraded to a best premium. The two wave off the diner menu on two occasions opting for various small appetizers, wine and conversation. When the waiter came over to replenish their wine glasses for the third time, he subtly bent over to Ed's left ear and whispered, "Mr. Ron has arrived and would like for you to join him in his private dining booth. I'll show you the way…sir if you will please follow me".

Ed found himself dumbstruck - this is not something he wants to end and glances at the waiter and says, "…Just give us a minute".

Linda, over-hearing Ed's conversation, says to the waiter, "…Is HE here, now?"; to which the waiter nods affirmably to Linda. "Fine", Linda says "I'll show Mr. Falconer the way…" and with that the waiter pulls back her chair and she nods with a smile to Ed. Ed finds himself speechless as the waiter assists with his chair, it is all he could do to keep from laughing – Ed is rarely 'scooped' and certainly not to this extent.

Linda folded her hand to the inside of Ed's arm and says, "I'll guide you …if you would like…" Ed's only response is "…please, show me the way…" and the two navigated between the tables to the very back of the restaurant towards a corner that Ed had not really seen before. The waiter pulls back the dark pastel curtains of a booth and revealed a dark red-carpeted entranceway with a very elegant door. The waiter then stepped in with them and closed the curtains, removed an old fashion key from his waist jacket, unlocked and opened the door and handed another key to Linda. Ed found himself standing in yet another entryway with another door. Linda turned to Ed and says "…sound-proofing" as she waited for the waiter to close the door behind them. Once the first door is closed a soft reddish light came on over the second door and Linda unlocks and opens the second door to reveal a large open space with card tables of Black-Jack, Poker and others, Ed sees a Rolette Wheel in a corner, with a number of slot machines against the wall. The gambling room is elegantly decorated with red carpet, chandler lighting and brass furnishings; the room is almost filled with noisy guests and it is all Ed could do as he felt 'scooped' once again.

Linda steered Ed, to the right where several elegant decorated dinner booths were located; and standing next to one of the larger booths is an imposing man that appeared to be a bodyguard.

As they approached the large man, Ed recognized him as Stephen and nods to him with a smile. Stephen is wearing dark glasses and did not return the smile. Ron is seated in the middle of the booth and did not bother to get up – but instead motioned them to either side of him. "So I see you've met Linda" Ron says as he kissed her on the cheek with a smile, then shook Ed's extended hand. Ed felt his thick muscular hand as he felt his grip. Ed thought this is a man who does his own work when other can't. One would not call Ron particularly handsome or attractive; rough features, short in stature – but extremely well dressed – with an unshaven look of the backwoods. Ron motions over the waiter with his cart of French Champagne and cheeses. "I've taken the liberty of ordering us some New England Lobster and Black Angus filets," Ron says without the usual look for approval. "I only eat fresh meat so I've waited until you arrived to have dinner prepared". Ed decides not to respond or to ask too many questions for he thought this is obviously Ron's party and everyone else were guests; but Ed did wonder if any other surprise guest would appear.

Ron entertains pleasantries in conversation about the area and how he had made his fortune in Emerald. He had designs to make much more with Ed's help. All through the dinner Ed and Linda listened while Ron extolled all the benefits that he had given to the community. Ed decides to smile and listen to Ron's conversation that is more like a monologue; and gave Linda some smiling looks as he enjoyed the dinner. As dinner ends, Ron decided that they all should have some Cognac, and discusses "business" then play the tables. Ed thought, finally...and raised an eyebrow to Linda. Ron then turned to Ed and abruptly says, "...so Ed... how do we make it all happen and when do I get my money?"

Ed had been waiting for this opportunity and says, "When can I see the product...?"

Ron responded sharply "What's the matter, don't you trust me...?" Ron responds and abruptly laughs. Then Ron proceeds to explain that Linda is Akiko's best friend and a kind of close friend of Derricks'. Ed looked at Ron with a puzzled expression of and so... "...Of Derrick and Paul's operation" Ron interjected. "OK let me explain" Ron continued "...Linda came to me with plants from Paul – that are the Amsterdam plants that you asked about; she told me that Paul is fed-up with Derrick and all his control and he wants out – and for big money he would deliver the Amsterdam plants and seeds. Paul is very much a recluse but I did talk to him and he confirmed that he wants out – but that he needs some big money to disappear".

Skeptical, Ed turns in his seat and looks over at Linda who hadn't said a word. "Look I have already lost one very trusted employee over this" Ed says firmly,

"THAT WAS AN Accident!" Ron says abruptly and pursed his lips with frustration.

"How do you know..." Ed cautiously says. Ron took a gulp of his cognac and motioned to the waiter for another round.

"Look Ed" Ron tries a softer approach "...Everyone knows everything in these parts…or at least the rumors of everything. I hear that your friend got lost in the mountains and his car broke down. The speculation was that he was some place he shouldn't of been…some grower helped him get his car out and the cable pulling the car snapped …knocking your employee to the ground…he hit his head on a rock and died…things like that happen around here…it is just an accident…" Ron finishes as he made circles on the top of his cognac glass while looking for the waiter.

"…But I hear that he ends up on some park entrance sign…?" Ed asked "…it is probably a grower that thought he is a Fed snooping around …and wanted to send a message" Ron responds casually and motions to Stephen to get the waiter. Ed stared down at the table and listens to Ron but could not get Michael out of his mind – what really did happen….

Ed wishes he had more time…and who is this Linda…and who is she with "You see that's the beauty of this project we already know what the product will bring…. and there is a ready-made market…". Ron sits there giving his sale pitch but Ed is only half listening and he had figured out where all this is going; but there were a few questions and all along Linda sits there with a smile. Ed looks at Linda who is looking back at him "…so how do you fit in all this…just so I have all the players in place…" Ed says abruptly and has decided to interrupt Ron during his droning sales pitch.

"…I brought the plants to Ron along with some of Paul's research papers… at least what I could find in his desk …I told Ron that I could probably could get more if they are worth anything" Linda says in a soft voice. Ed thought …I like the way she talks, straight forward. "…So you want a piece of the action as well…?" Ed asked pointedly; Ron attempted to interrupt, but Ed says "I'd like to hear it from her". As Ed is listening to Linda's remarks he noticed the Maître d from the corner of his eye motioning toward their table. Then a waiter came walking briskly towards Stephen and Stephen turns to one side away from Ed. Stephen bends slightly downward to the waiter and still the waiter had to stand on his tip toes. Ed sees the waiter whisper something to Stephen then stand away from Stephen. Stephen looks over at Ron and stares until he had Ron's attention.

At this point Ron is beginning to feel shutout, which is something that you just don't do with Ron.

Ron looks over at Stephen who had nodded his head towards Ron and put a finger to his ear. Ron abruptly motions for Ed to move out of the booth so he could leave the booth. Ed moved out and then says, "…Ron, you don't mind if I sit closer to Linda so we can chat…do you"? Ed at this point is not much interested in what Ron's response is but he did hear Ron say,

"Fine…whatever…" as Ed is already moving into the center spot of the table where Ron had been sitting. Ron disappeared around the corner from the Maitre 'd.

Ron goes to a phone near the Maitre 'd booth and abruptly says to the Maitre 'd "transfer the call to the downstairs office" and slammed the phone down and abruptly left, walking through the Casino floor. Once in Ron's office, the desk is covered in paperwork and in a semi-organized fashion in various size piles; Ron picked up the phone says in a very low and angry voice "THIS BETTER BE GOOD!!"

It is Kyle with Frank sounding very nervous – Ron listens intensely chewing on a toothpick while popping small bits of candy in his mouth. "Kyle wants money, a lot of money, enough to get out of Emerald and disappear further up north". Ron paused for what seems for Kyle to be too much time – but then Ron came back – "I'll give you the money and trade for your place – sign over a 'quick claim' and nail it to your front door – but you still have to finish up the real job I asked you to do….". Ron listened as Kyle tried to figure out how to get the money without Ron's people getting him. Ron turns toward the wall and quietly says in a low stern voice "…I won't come after you as long as you completely clear out …. Look you and Tom are close, … you go see Tom. He'll have the money for you …and yes another half for Frank, although he never did anything but handle…YES…YES …it will be there by the time you get there…!" Ron slams the phone down and pushed the phone buttons for Tom's place…

✻ ✻ ✻ ✻ ✻

Ed had decided that the game had changed and now he held the upper hand; everyone seemed to want something from him. Ed looks at Linda and says "... And so you where saying…?" as he moved in closer to Linda. Ed is nothing if he isn't a 'ladies man' even though he figured he is probably 15 years her senior; but he thought he wanted to play this through….What's the worse that could happen…he'd find out Linda is Ron's mistress or something and end up with his head falling on a rock….Ed quickly shook the thought from his head. He looks at Linda and she is smiling back at him not so much with her eyes but he sees it in her eyes – and then he knew. "Look, all I know is that Ron asked me to meet him here…that he had some business deal that would help us both…" Linda says in flirtatious manner that had Ed a little put off but it put smile on his face… however, he did appreciate that it is cute.

As faith, would have it just then, Ed could see Ron returning from the corner of his eye and he had a fancy decanter and a glass. Ed nods his head in Ron's direction and Linda lowers her head and Ed moves just slightly away from her.

"Now don't you two look cozy …getting to know each other…?" Ron says with a stupid grin on his face that spoke only of sex. "You know Ed, AS I WAS ABOUT TO SAY before I was interrupted, now that Linda has broken up with Paul she's available…!" Ron says with that stupid grin again. Linda softly smiled back at Ed, and the smile in her eyes is faded there.

"Well…so who has these research papers and when can I see them… and where's this plant?" Ed says firmly but in a matter of fact way.

"As soon as we have an understanding…. and some good-faith money for us." Ron responded with that wider grin that showed his gold back molar tooth; which told Ed far more than he really wanted to know.

Ed gave a firm "NO" and then says "if we are going to do business I need to see what the value is and work out how much the company can make." Ed pauses and glances at Linda "…from our arrangement" Ed finishes and helps himself to the decanter that Ron had brought back with him …and refilled Linda's glass. Ed continued, "Remy XO, I prefer the Hine …but this is very good".

Ron interrupted saying "Remy XO Private Reserve" with the slightest of smile; Ed nods.

"…. Private Reserve…I stand corrected" Ed says in his best old school charm he could muster; which very nearly caused Linda to bust out in laughter – she quickly covered her mouth and Ed knew that they were on the same page.

"Well with no car or transportation I guess I'm here for the duration, so let's make the best of it…. Ron its your show…so let's proceed" Ed says in a matter of fact voice – feeling confident that he is going to get the real story from Linda.

"Finally…" Ron responds in an irritated voice; and told Stephen to grab the decanter and meet them in his office. "Stephen will show you the way; I'll be there shortly" Ron says as he started to scoot out of the booth. "I have some business to attend to" Ron says as he left them.

Ed and Linda followed Stephen through a dimly lit hallway to a freight elevator. Stephen put a card key into the panel and then pressed the top button. The elevator jerked and Linda is about to lose her balance; when Ed grabbed her elbow "…freight elevators often give an unexpected ride…lean on the back wall – just in case the ride becomes more than we expected" Ed says – helping Linda to regain her balance and putting his arm around her waist. Linda looked at Ed's arm around her waist "…just wanted to make sure you would be safe" Ed responds; and Linda gave him a whimsical smile.

The elevator ride is indeed not as smooth as one would expect for business guests but then this is unusual business. Ed smiles at Linda while he calculated in his head the value Ron would gain – he knew he had a large piece of the marijuana market; but Ed realized that all Ron wanted is to have a level market with Derrick – unless the stories about Ron are true. Kyle had emphasized to Ed that Ron is not a man to underestimate or cross; a jealous man of all his property including women. Kyle told him a story of how Ron had his mistress killed because he thought she was having an affair; then told everyone that she is a snoop for the Feds. What Ed did not realize is that Kyle had carried out the deeds – leaving her hanging in an apartment with her child in the room and how Ron had everything planned to the smallest detail – even having the room cleaned before her body is discovered.

The elevator stops in front of a doorway; Stephen pulled out a key and unlocked the door. The room had been pretty much what Ed had expected – decorated in a business manner - dark wood (probably Mahogany – Ed thought); expensive chairs and a beautiful leather couch and of course the larger than life wooden desk. Ed thought that given Ron's stature he should of chosen a smaller desk and Ed smiled at the thought. Ed noticed that Linda looks nervous as if she had never been in the office or seen such a cold immaculately decorated business office – Ed glances around, and as he expected, there, on the wall in the back were heads of a Buffalo, Elk and some sort of large cat or perhaps a Mountain lion. Ed nodded to the animals' head at Linda – who just gave a skirmish grin and looks into Ed's eyes – there is that smile Ed is glad to see.

Ron enters the room from another entrance and Ed gave an '…I'm not surprised look to Linda'. Stephen had disappeared when Ron entered after a short conversation that gave Ron a Cheshire cat grin.

Ron says "…sit…sit" motioning over to the couch with the animal heads over it

Ed says "…I think we all would be more comfortable with the chairs at your desk or perhaps over by that coffee table. We could move a few chairs around… perhaps you could place the plants on the coffee table so I can examine it". Just then Stephen appeared – Ed had barely noticed that he had left – he is pushing a chrome dinner cart with a single small plant on the top along with a folder – which Ed assumed is the papers that Linda had discussed.

"Fine…fine…whatever…" Ron responded in an irritated voice. Stephen placed the chairs around a fine glass top coffee table on what appeared to be a large Redwood burl.

Stephen poured the cognac keeping everyone's glass replenished; while Ed examined the papers and gave a glancing look at the small marijuana plant in a ten inch plastic pot, while Linda sits pensive in her chair. In short order Ed says "…this is out of my league …I'm just an Exec who helps Quantex sell their product", which brought a chuckle from Ron. "Look do we have a deal…I know that Quantex has to be interested in this plant's capability – the highest THC quantity and quality – just the ease of the product production would be worth a great deal…. I'll supply the raw product for you… Quantex does whatever with it …and we all we all can be living large…" Ron commented.

"… Why do I need you, I could just as easily do business with Derrick who probably has more product than you right now…" Ed responded in a matter of fact business tone; which brought a red face and angry look from Ron. Ed thought '…here we go – now we can get down to business'.

Ron got up for his chair grabbing Ed's arm and walked over to his desk; Linda started to follow – to which Stephen walked in front of her and politely asked her to stay seated.

Ed is taken back by Ron's firm grip on his arm, but followed along, glancing at Linda who looks very concerned. Ed knew then that this is all unexpected by her. Ed pulls at his arm expecting Ron to release his grip but it didn't happen. Ron sat Ed in a chair in front of his desk and bent down whispering in Ed's ear; "… Derrick is not going to be around much longer…" and finished with "…accidents do happen around here…". Ron sat on the edge of his desk; his feet dangling off the floor – which in itself almost brought a chuckle from Ed – but he surmised this is not the time or the place.

Ron looks angrily at Ed and says "…I CONTROL WHAT HAPPENS AROUND HERE….I produce far more product than anyone …Derrick is a hobbyist that just sells enough to support his operation…and I can make trouble for whomever I please…". Ron is looking at Ed with the face of a man who meant what he says – and Ed had no doubt of his veracity.

"OK…ok…I have to ask… what kind of GOOD FAITH money were you thinking about".

To which Ron says without missing a beat "A MILLION…to start with then we can talk product cost".

Ed knew that Ron is serious and had expected a figure that would test his resolve, and responded with "I can write you a check right now for $300,000".

Ron sternly responded with "…ok $850,000 and I'll throw in all of Paul's paperwork that I can get my hands on – hell, I'll send you his desk" and gave a cold chuckle meant to send a chill down Ed's back.

Ed calmly says "…I can write you a check for $500,000 now …that is my limit…and we can negotiate the rest after my people have a look at all this but we want the production".

Ron responded "NO PAPERWORK…until we have a deal…and I want an agreement that you guys will not try to re-produce any plants …THAT IS MY END".

Ed responded with "DONE and I'll take the plant with me….";

Ron quickly responded with a chuckle "DONE…but you can't get that plant on a plane…".

ED says "let me worry about that" and got up from his chair shaking Ron's hand with deal.

Ed sits down beside Ron's desk and pulls out his briefcase from under the desk where his chair is. Ron didn't look surprised as Ed took the briefcase and pulled out his company check folder. "You know you both have to stay here until that check clears my bank…." Ron says with a smile.

Ed responded "…I assume you have control of a bank around here …so that this won't take very long".

Ron nodded with a smile and says "…you know this is just my part …you still have Linda's piece to take care of…"

Ed quickly responded "I'll talk with Linda about that…unless she wants you as her agent…"

Ed looks over at Linda who says, "I can take care of myself …thank you very much…".

Ed hands Ron his check and gulps his glass of cognac…and says "…does Stephen show us to our rooms …or are we free to get our own room keys".

Ron pulls two room card keys from his desk and says, "…you can use the front elevator…I'll let you know when the check clears". Ed just smiles and then looks over to Linda who is following Stephen toward the elevator that Ron had used.

Ed examines the Card keys and sees that their rooms were next to each other smiling with the thought "well at least he knew that Linda is not his mistress". But his age is catching up with him as he wearily thought; '…this is what I hired Michael to do…this is becoming all to much'.

The two left the elevator on the fourth floor; Ed walking with Linda thinking '…a younger Ed would have her pinned her against the wall…grabbing her butt and encouraging her to pull off his jacket …while he unbuttoned her dress'. Ed smiles to Linda and gave her a polite but weary smile…as she stops at her door….. .

Linda turns to Ed and says with a smile "I hear the breakfast is great…".

Ed responds, "…how about we go somewhere local".

Linda says with a smile in her eyes "I know just the place" and unlocks her door and smiles at Ed as he wearily walks to his adjacent room door.

Ed closes the room door, kicks off his shoes and collapses on the bed; as he is trying to contemplate whether to fall asleep in his clothes or…he hears a knock on the door that opens to Linda's adjacent room. Ed thinks 'how do you tell a beautiful woman… No…Ed thought this would be a first'. Ed opens the door and there she is with those smiley eyes and in a bathrobe. As Ed is about to say how tired he is…Linda says "you must really be beat…I just want to tell you that I admire the way you handled Ron…I have never seen Ron in action …but wow…you just seem to …well…to handle him…just want to say thank you… and I am very worried." With that Linda gave Ed a kiss on the cheek…and there is that smile…as Linda began to turn away she says "…People around here say that my massages are the best….I bet I could have you asleep in no time…" Ed smiles and is trying to think of a response when Linda grabs his hand and pulls him into her room.

She says with a smile …"I have hot bath water…I can give you a massage while you are soaking …unless you are too shy." Ed tries to think of the right words. Linda says "you really are beat huh…go in the bathroom take off your clothes and I'll be there in a minute".

All that Ed could manage is "look I really thank you but….."

And with that Linda says with a smile " its just a massage if you fall sleep I'll make sure you don't drown and put you to bed…" and she took Ed's arm and gave him a gentle shove toward her bathroom. True to her word, Ed sees a warm soap bubble bath with steam rising….

Ed smiles and says " oh well don't be surprised if I fall asleep on you" .

She responds, "I'm counting on it".

The bath water is soothing and he felt the warmth take over his body; Linda is still in her bathrobe and she is right it is the best massage. … Either that or he is too tired to care. Everywhere she touched… the muscles just seem to surrender to her touch. As he is almost sleep, he heard her say.. "No…drowning …please…. you shower off and I'll put you to bed". Ed obeyed her command and thought where were you ten years ago…I could of saved myself a lonely divorce.

Ed showers and puts on his robe…and then sees Linda standing beside her bed still in her bathrobe …. Ed smiles and heads for the adjoining room door. Linda grabs his hand …and says, "the best part of my massages is that people always fall into the best sleep" and she pulls him to her bed. He tries to protest – well not very hard – to which she responds…"its just a massage …and I have to make sure the hero sleeps well…I promise it is just a massage" with that Ed climbs into bed nude and Linda had him lay on his stomach.

Linda climbed on to Ed's back, her legs straddling either side of him. Ed could feel that she didn't have any clothes on under her …but all he could do is smile as once again his muscles surrender to her touch. Ed thought if I told any one about this they would never believe it …and true to her words Ed drifted into a deep sleep.

CHAPTER 15

GRANITE MARKER FIRE

Ed woke from his sound sleep as he stretched he sees that Linda unfortunately is not there. He heard her voice in the bathroom but only just barely as she softly spoke into her cell phone. As Ed got up to listen, the floorboard creaked and Linda closed the bathroom door. Ed thinks he would try to listen in but thought better of it since they hadn't really …well been formally introduced …and the thought brought an almost chuckle to him. He thought, this is the time for gentleman like conduct and put on the robe that is laying at the end of the bed. As Ed put the robe on, the thought crossed his mind 'just maybe she has done this before…'.

Linda emerged from the bathroom in a very slinky dark blue mid-thigh pajama skirt…Ed thought 'sexy but she has that nervous look' that Ed thought he had seen in her when she is talking about Ron last night. Linda sits on Ed's side of the bed …Ed thought looks like a conversation is about to happen …so he sat down beside her – to get a real feel for the conversation – after all the pajama top had a very nice 'V' that showed her cleavage and her naked breast definitely gave a nice shape to her top…. As Ed sits down and went to put his arm around her, she turned facing toward him…taking his hand and putting it on her knee.

She says "yes…but we have to talk…". Ed thought women in the morning, they just don't understand, but he looks at her patiently. "I need breakfast," she says abruptly …and Ed thought huh…! "I have to have breakfast…I have this thing…well ….I just have to have breakfast…since I gave up smoking ….I just have to have breakfast".

Ed smiled again patiently and says I'll call room service…

She says "NO…NO…I don't want to eat here…. I know this place very near here…just down the road in 'Richardson Groove'. …They have the best country ham and pancakes…and I feel like pancakes…. ".

Ed looks at her in puzzlement and is about to suggest – the café in Barber – when Linda says, "YES…Richardson Groove…OK?" Ed felt compelled in someway and just responded "Then Richardson Grove it is …" she looked at him and says "…trust me …you'll love it….". Ed thought a strange choice of words but got up after giving her thigh a gentle squeeze – and then thought 'oh my she has a shape'.

Ed then heads off to his room to see about something to wear – after-all Ron did say that they brought everything over. As he entered the room he heard Linda yell to him "…Can we just get dressed and leave now…ah…we can clean-up later – after-all this is the backcountry".

Ed thought about protesting …but decided that would probably be useless. Then he sees the car keys … on the top of his bed; he turns and she is standing there smiling in the doorway…Ed sees that the way the sunlight caught her, he could just …almost see her shape…and the even looking fresh out of bed … hair…it is all Ed could do but smile …and she says. " It's the dark blue Audi, parked around the side …near the kitchen entrance…I'll be down in just a min-ute"…and she is gone..

Ed thought that maybe she is trying to avoid Ron … and just did not want to talk about it …after all it is early morning and Ed is betting that Ron is a late sleeper.

✳ ✳ ✳ ✳ ✳

Lee sat at his usual place in the diner …but he had asked Marge to hold the back table open; he hardly heard the conversation and the guys' thought something is up. Lee heard "So I heard you did some fast driving …all over creation…?"

Lee looked up and as the question is repeated… Lee is looking for something that would do for an answer … he sees Sarah coming in the front door… and says, "Excuse me fellows but my breakfast date is here…" and with that he scoots out of the booth and motions to Sarah.

As they sat down in the back booth, Lee couldn't help but notice Sarah seeming nervous. Lee had asked Sarah to join him because he knew that something is going on and wanted to see if she knew anything – and for this conversation he need more than the telephone. Lee had Donnie filling out the EPA forms that were now substantially over due. Sarah made a point of sitting facing the doorway…and smiled pleasantly at Lee, while he looked around the diner.

Juan walked over to wipe down the table – and Lee thought it odd because he had seen Sally wipe it down earlier just after she came back from her break – to go see Donnie – Lee imagines. Juan gave Sarah a look – then glances over at the clock and turned to walk away. Sarah says "I'll just go wash my hands before we have breakfast".

Sarah scooted out the booth and walks towards the restroom; Lee could see her stop to talk to Juan before she entered the restroom.

When Sarah came back Lee asked "What's Juan up to these days?" But Sarah just brushed the question aside as Sally walked up to take their order.

Sarah just says coffee and toast and didn't seem to have her usual pleasant conversation and smile with Sally. After Sally left, Lee knew something is going on and turned to Sarah and looked straight into her eyes; "OK" Sarah says, "… You just have to trust me …" and talked about the shop that is going to be vacant in Barber…. ".

Lee smiles and greets Sally as she came back with their order. When Sally had left, Sarah turns to Lee and says very softly "Ron is pissed off at Derrick …something about that guy from Quantex…I think there is going to be trouble". Lee says,

"…You mean there IS going to be trouble…". Sarah took Lee's hand and put his hand on her thigh under the table and says "Shhhh…whatever happens you just need to let it play out…" and squeezed Lee's hand.

Sarah and Lee were finishing up their breakfast when Donnie called Lee on his cell phone; Donnie is yelling into the phone "THERE'S a big fire at The Park side entrance over by the Granite Marker; county fire is on their way and they'd ask the Park Service to send their trucks – they say you can see it from Barber its so big".

Just then, Bob bursts in the doorway yelling at Lee. "The Park at the side entrance is on fire right at the granite stone marker". The diner emptied like the café is on fire - people running to their trucks and down to Bob's Used Car lot to see if they could see it. Lee got up and Sarah grabbed his hand;

Lee says, "I have to see what I can do…" Sarah gave Lee a grim smile and Lee is gone. Sarah sat at the booth and looks at Juan as he came over to clear the table.

Juan says "I'm sure everything will be all right" Sarah nods as tears ran down her cheeks. Marge came over and put her arm around Sarah and they sat in the empty café as Juan looked over at them.

✳ ✳ ✳ ✳ ✳

Linda quickly got into the passenger side of the car and she says "Just head south on the highway you'll see the GROVE on your right – we should go quickly …I am hungry…and you don't want to see me get grouchy…"

Linda smiled and put Ed's hand on her thigh Ed says. "Yes love" and sped off to the Grove.

CHAPTER 16

WINTER AGAIN

The next winter is bitter cold and all the talk is about medical Marijuana – most of the growers were upset about it – there goes all the profits – and they met in groups to figure how they could make sure that marijuana isn't legalized. All over Emerald the people were talking legalized marijuana and how they were finally going to get control of the money – "we'll tax the shit out of it – get our schools – the way they should be" some were looking for more of a partnership after all. The growers had built a Town Hall, paid for a water system and gave funds for the Barber street repairs.

Lee sat in his usual seat in the café – with Donnie and the guys …and they begrudgingly let Sarah join them. Not much had changed that year – just the promise of change. Everyone still waited for the results from the Amsterdam Marijuana Cup. Only this year there is sadness because they knew Derrick and Paul weren't going to be there. The town paper brought in a special edition of the Independent – announcing the winner – some guys from the north part of the Emerald Triangle – but the real news is the test results from the Quantex Lab – just like last year some unknown person had dropped-off a small plant and a bud that broke the record THC level from the year before.

There is a back page piece about the State and Federal trials that Ron is fighting – the legal fees are costing Ron millions – some say they would never be able to prove any connection with the fire at Derrick's farm or any of the mysterious deaths that had happen in and round Baber . Everyone thought the State was crazy to try and get a conviction on murder. Everyone had enough of Ron anyway after he tried to distribute weed that he claimed came from the secret Amsterdam Cup – "Highest THC" ever he says – Everyone sat at the table curious to see what is in the box that Lee had brought with him – all the way from France.

Lee undid the packaging and extra wrap – to discover a bottle of wine D&P Vineyards France with a note that read – "HAPPY ANNIVERSARY". Lee looked puzzled and Sarah smiled saying the bottle says wine produced from France and "Distributed by Falconer Inc, NYC." Donnie reminded the group "…isn't that the name of the guy from the Pharmacy Company that was here last year?"

Sarah says, "… Shhhh … that is Linda's car that ended at the bottom of Snake Canyon in the river. And someone else says just a shame that there isn't a body to bury – I think both of them did right by this community.

They passed the paper around "Hey, says here Global Warming is going to bring us a colder winter."

The End
to be continued….